Infinity

GABRIEL JOSIPOVICI was born in Nice in 1940 of Russo-Italian, Romano-Levantine parents. He lived in Egypt from 1945 to 1956, when he came to Britain. After graduating from Oxford he joined the faculty of the University of Sussex in 1963, where he remained till he took early retirement in 1998. He is the author of sixteen novels, three volumes of short stories, eight critical works, a memoir of his mother, the poet and translator Sacha Rabinovitch, and numerous stage and radio plays, and is a regular contributor to the *Times Literary Supplement*. His work has been translated into the major European languages and Arabic. Visit www.gabrieljosipovici.org for further information.

Also by Gabriel Josipovici

Fiction
The Inventory (1968)
Words (1971)
Mobius the Stripper: Stories and Short Plays (1974)
The Present (1975)
Four Stories (1977)
Migrations (1977)
The Echo Chamber (1979)
The Air We Breathe (1981)
Conversations in Another Room (1984)
Contre Jour: A Triptych after Pierre Bonnard (1986)
In the Fertile Land (1987)
Steps: Selected Fiction and Drama (1990)
The Big Glass (1991)
In a Hotel Garden (1993)
Moo Pak (1994)
Now (1998)
Goldberg: Variations (2002)
Everything Passes (2006)
Two Novels: After and Making Mistakes (2009)
Heart's Wings (2010)

Theatre
Vergil Dying (1977)

Non-fiction
The World and the Book (1971, 1979)
The Lessons of Modernism (1977, 1987)
Writing and the Body (1982)
The Mirror of Criticism: Selected Reviews (1983)
The Book of God: A Response to the Bible (1988, 1990)
Text and voice: Essays 1981-1991 (1992)
A Life (2001)
The Singer on the Shore: Essays 1991-2004 (2006)
What Ever Happened to Modernism? (2010)
(ed.) *The Modern English Novel: The Reader, the Writer and the Book* (1975)
(ed.) *The Siren's Song: Selected Essays of Maurice Blanchot* (1980)
(ed. with Brian Cummings) *The Spirit of England: Selected Essays of Stephen Medcalf* (2010)

GABRIEL JOSIPOVICI

Infinity
The Story of a Moment

CARCANET

Acknowledgement

An extract from this work was first published in issue 34 of *The Reader* (Summer 2009).

First published in Great Britain in 2012 by
Carcanet Press Limited
Alliance House
Cross Street
Manchester M2 7AQ

www.carcanet.co.uk

ISBN 978 1 84777 166 7

The publisher acknowledges financial assistance from Arts Council England

Typeset in Monotype Centaur by XL Publishing Services, Tiverton
Printed and bound in England by SRP Ltd, Exeter

To Jonathan Harvey

— How do you wish me to go on?

— Describe him.

— He was very tall and thin, at least he gave the impression of being very tall, though to tell the truth he was not above medium height, perhaps even a little less, with an aquiline nose and, in those days, when I first went to work for him, black hair, so black it was almost blue, if you know what I mean, sir. The kind of black that could, in certain lights, be blue.

— Go on.

— All of us Italians have black hair, except of course for those who are blond, but Sicilians have blacker hair than most, if you know what I mean, sir.

— Yes, I understand. Now go on.

— Yes, sir. He always dressed very expensively. He had over a hundred suits in his cupboards, it was up to me to see that the moths did not get at them and that they remained clean and fresh, for he might at any moment of the day or night, for he sometimes worked through the night and sometimes he would spend the night walking through the streets of Rome, decide to put one of them on. It was up to me to see that they were always ready to be put on, so that if he had worn one once I would have to make sure it was cleaned and pressed before it was put back in the cupboard, in case he wanted to take it out again soon. And it was the same with his shirts. He told me that when he was living in Vienna in the 1930s, when he was studying composition with Walter Scheler, he always sent his suits to London to be dry-cleaned, and his shirts too, to be washed and pressed. Only London, he said, has the requisite standards of cleaning and pressing, only the English upper classes know what it means to have a properly pressed suit of clothes. Of course, he said, that is no longer the case. Nowadays the English upper classes are on the run, he said, they are being hunted down one by one. In England the hunting of wild animals is being abolished little by little, he said, but the hunting of the English aristocracy is being pursued with ever greater ferocity. The English were once the most civilised people in the world, he said, but they are now among the most barbaric. The French are the only civilised people left, he said. They are resisting the barbarism of America, the barbarism of the New World, but they will not be able to resist for ever. Soon nobody will know what the word civilisation means. We must turn away from the world, as the Hindu sages have long known, he said, because the world will never be able to live up to our idea of what the world should be. We must practise every day, he said, every day, Massimo, in order to eradicate our desire to make the world a better and more civilised place, we must learn to accept that it will only ever be a worse and less civilised place. Soon, he said, even the memory of past civilisation will have disappeared, not in your lifetime, Massimo, he said, and certainly not in mine, but very soon, very soon. We have reached the end of the Neolithic period, Massimo, he said. It is only now that we have reached the end of the Neolithic. Your children, Massimo, he said, will no longer know that milk is produced by cows, they will not even know what a cow is. They will only know what a self-service supermarket is, which is the place where they can buy milk. So we are entering a new era, he said. After the end of the Neolithic we have come to the era of the Synthetic. No one will know what a stone is any more, no one will know what a tree is, no one will know what a flower is, no one will know the mathematical symbol for infinity. But why should we care?

does not walk but he rolls. I met many such rollers when I was in India and Nepal, he said. It did not matter to them how long it took to reach their destination. It did not matter if it took them a year or five years or a whole lifetime. They took the cloth from around their shoulders and held it in their hands stretched out above their heads as they rolled to stop themselves falling into ditches. It gave them equilibrium. Equilibrium, Massimo, he said, is the essential condition for rolling. Without equilibrium you keep ending up in the ditch and you never advance at all. But once you find equilibrium, he said, you can roll for many miles every day. Try it, Massimo, he said. Try it in your spare time. You will discover that it is almost impossible to roll in a straight line. That is the reason for the cloth, Massimo, he said, by holding a cloth above your head stretched between both hands you can manage to roll in a straight line, or in an almost straight line, though the bruising to your elbows and upper arms has to be seen to be believed. Sometimes the bruising and the cuts to the arms and to the legs and to the body as well is so bad and the wounds become so infected that they have to stop, sometimes for months on end, in order to recover. But they always go on, Massimo, he said, they always go on. Usually, he said they have a man walking ahead of them, whose task is to sweep the ground ahead of them to remove the roughest stones and also to remove the ants and worms and other insects, for it would never do to trample on an ant or a worm while rolling. An ant or a worm, he said, are as worthy of life as any human being. The essential thing to understand is that what gives your life its special quality, without which you are nothing, is the recognition that you are worth as much or as little as any ant or worm. Once you have understood that,

Massimo, he said, all the rest follows. To roll for thousands of miles through swamp and desert, through cities and over mountains and to trample and crush to death spiders and ants and beetles and gnats on the way is worse than not to go on pilgrimage at all, so a man goes before you, whether it is in swamp or desert, in the city or over the mountain, and he sweeps the ground clear of any living thing and you roll behind him, minute after minute and hour after hour and day after day and month after month and year after year, and in the end you reach your goal, you reach the goal of your pilgrimage, which is the shrine of the holy man. I met many such rollers in my brief stay in India and Nepal, he said, and I have to say they made a vivid impression on me.

He was silent.

After a while I said: Go on.

— Yes sir, he said. How would you like me to go on?

— In any way you wish, I said.

— Yes sir, he said, but he did not go on.

— Did he often speak about his wife? I finally asked.

— Not often, he said, but sometimes. When I got to know him better, when he began to take me into his confidence.

— What did he say?

— He said she was the most beautiful woman he had ever met. Beauty is not to be despised, Massimo, he said. Though it is a gift like any other and has not been earned, it is nevertheless a gift, and as such should be celebrated. He had met many beautiful women, he said, and he had had affairs with quite a few of them. It is always a disaster, he said, but it should never be a cause for regret. Beauty is a gift, he said, but it is also a curse. It is a curse on the person who is the beneficiary of that gift and it is a curse on whoever comes into contact with them. Because the person who is beautiful does not know where that gift came from and cannot relate it to herself. So she sees herself in the mirror and she falls in love with herself, but she does not know who this person is that she has fallen in love with and she spends her life trying to find out. She hopes that the men who come under her spell will be able to reveal this to her, and when she finds that they are as much in the dark about it as she is herself she grows angry and disappointed and looks for another man to explain it to her. But the men are attracted to her beauty precisely because it is inexplicable and beyond reason. They are like moths around a flame and sooner or later they fly too near and then the flame catches them and they shrivel up and die. That is why beautiful women are always tense, he said, and why they are always capricious and changeable. They do not know their own minds, he said. They try to live with this beauty and they cannot. They cannot live with it and they cannot ignore it, so they live in perpetual puzzlement and frustration, making little darts into the world in the hope of catching it unawares, but finding only that they have been disappointed once again. The first beautiful woman I fell in love with, Massimo, he said, was my cousin Lara. I watched her little breasts bud and then grow and I would willingly have given my life to see her naked and to pass my hand over them. But I did not need to give my life, he said, she was only too willing to show them to me and to let me pass my hand over them for nothing. I thought I had reached heaven, he said, but she soon found that my caresses did not give her what she thought she was looking for and the next time I touched her she slapped my face. I should have learned my lesson then, Massimo, he said, but it was to take me another thirty years and many more such pains and disappointments before I finally did so.

He was silent.

— Go on, I said.

— Yes sir, he said.

Since he still seemed disinclined to do so I asked him: Did he often speak to you like that?

— Like what, sir?

— About such... intimate things.

— Not at the beginning, of course, he said, but later on, when he understood how reliable I was and how much I admired and respected him. Then he would talk to me about everything under the sun. Especially when we went out driving into the Campagna. Even about music, though he knew I was quite ignorant on the subject.

— What did he say?

— About what?

— About music.

— He talked. You know how it is, sir.

— But I am asking you.

— About music?

— Yes.

— Each sound is a sphere, he said. It is a sphere, Massimo, and every sphere has a centre. The centre of the sound is the heart of the sound. One must always strive to reach the heart of the sound, he said. If one can reach that one is a true musician. Otherwise one is an artisan. To be an artisan is perfectly respectable, Massimo, he said. Even to be an artisan of music is respectable. But it must not be confused with being a musician. A musician is not an artisan, he said. He is an intermediary.

That is a completely different thing. It entails a completely different way of understanding music and a completely different way of understanding ourselves. A completely different way. If you do not know the difference between a craft and a calling, he said, you do not know what it means to be an artist. Today, he said, very few people know what it means to be an artist. Very few artists know what it means to be an artist. They want to have their photographs taken in order to show off their noses. But we all have noses, he said, and few people are artists. True artists. They want to show off their profiles and tell the newspapers how wonderful they are. But they are not wonderful, they are only human beings and they are worse than most human beings because they are prostituting their gifts. That's what he said. Prostituting their gifts. If they had any gifts in the first place, he said. Most of the time they have no gifts at all but only the desire to show off their profiles and to talk to the newspapers. The art is incidental, he said, what is important is to show off your nose and talk to the papers. To tell them what your ideas are and why you are so special. That is what the newspapers want, he said. They want to take photographs of their profiles and to hear how special they are. They want to hear about how much you feel and what happened to you in your childhood. They want to hear about your political views and your views of the Church. If your nose is not the right sort of nose you can forget the newspapers, he said. You can forget the festivals. You can forget the commissions. You can forget the recording companies. I have never wanted to have my nose photographed, he said. My nose is handsomer and more distinguished than most of theirs, he said. It is a Sicilian nose. An aristocratic nose. But it is not for the papers, he said. It is not for the publicity brochures. It is solely for me, so as to enable me to breathe and to work. A musician is primarily a worker, he said. He is not a clothes horse. He is not a politician. He is not a philosopher. He is not a lover. He is a worker. I have hired you, Massimo, he said, to get my travel tickets when I want to go somewhere or to drive me out into the countryside when I need to escape the town. But above all I need someone to keep the newspaper reporters and the photographers from my door. You cannot imagine, he said, the degree of laziness, venality and mendacity of these journalists. Not so long ago, he said, when I attended the premiere of a work of mine in Paris, all the journalists could say was: 'Mr Pavone does not do things by halves, not only does he write an entire work on one note, but he sleeps not in a bed but in a cupboard.' Can you imagine, Massimo? he said, not in a bed but in a cupboard. What had happened, he said, was this. He was installed in one of the best hotels in Paris, the Raphael. Unfortunately his room was situated not far from the lifts, so that the first night he hardly got any sleep at all. The next day, after he had complained, they gave him another room. Not just another room, he said to me, but the best room, nothing less than the royal suite. The bed alone, he said, was the size of most hotel rooms, and had a pair of steps next to it so as to help you climb into it. After a long day of rehearsals and seeing friends, he retired to his room, utterly exhausted. But no sooner had I climbed the steps and crawled into the bed and put out the light, he said, than I became aware of a humming noise filling the room. At first I tried to ignore it, he said, but it grew so insistent that I had no option but to turn on the light and descend the steps and see if I could locate the source of the noise. And indeed I did, he said, it emanated from a pipe which was located about a metre beneath my window. I shut the window tight, he said, and drew the curtains, and tried to go to sleep, but though for a while I thought I had managed to shut out the noise it was soon filling my ears again. I got up and went into the bathroom, where I found some cotton wool, which I stuffed into my ears. Once again I climbed the steps and snuggled down deep under my eiderdown, hoping that at last I would be able to sleep. But even there the noise found me out, and soon I was wide awake, my heart pounding dangerously in my chest. I determined not to panic, however, he said, so I put on the light again and surveyed my surroundings. Against the wall opposite the window stood an enormous cupboard, the kind used for storing bedsheets and blankets. I opened it and indeed it was full of sheets and blankets. I took some of them out and lay down on the rest. I found I could stretch out, so I returned to the bed, collected my pillow and eiderdown and settled down in the cupboard for the night. However, though with the cupboard door shut I could no longer hear the offending hum, it was also unbearably stuffy, so that I had to keep opening the door to let in some air and then closing it again to shut out the noise. You can imagine what kind of a night I had, he said. However, buoyed up by the thought of the performance, the next day I leapt out of my improvised bed and hurried down to breakfast. The chambermaid must have come in, discovered my pillow and eiderdown in the cupboard, guessed that my bed had not been slept in and alerted the papers. The only thing they could find to say about me was that I wrote music on one note and slept in cupboards. These people are monsters, Massimo, he said. They must be kept out at all costs. That is why I hired someone like you, he said, someone who has no trouble lifting the rear ends of cars to look underneath them, to inspect their rear parts, so to speak. What a musician needs is peace and time, he said, peace and time, inner peace and inner time. He needs quiet and he needs to be alone. If someone does not like to be alone he should not become an artist, he said. Today writing music is incidental to the life of a musician. Writing music is a necessary evil, undertaken solely in order to generate the photographs and the interviews and the dinners and the invitations to festivals. Every musician will tell you, Massimo, he said, that he lives only for his music, but that is not true. If he believes that, he is only fooling himself. He lives to get his nose in the newspapers and to be applauded and worshipped wherever he goes. That is worse than cleaning the gutters, he said. A real musician, Massimo, he said, should be able to clean the gutters, he should be able to fight in the trenches, he should be able to work in an office or a hospital, because he has made a space for solitude inside himself where the music will be written.

— What did he mean, I asked him, by a space for solitude inside himself?

— I don't know, he said.

— He did not explain?

— You know how it is, sir. Mr Pavone talked and I listened. Especially when I was driving.

— Of course. Go on.

— Especially in later years, sir, he said, he would ask me to drive him out into the Campagna. Then he would talk. I think he felt the need to talk. Drive, Massimo, drive, he would say. If we are hungry we will stop somewhere for a bite to eat. Sometimes he was completely silent, he was thinking about his music. He would close his eyes and sit back in his seat. I could see him out of the corner of my eye. Sometimes he would make a little noise, a hum or a bark or something like la-la-la. Sometimes he would pass his hand in front of his face or make a movement of his hand as if he was trying to hold something. Then he would be still again for a long time. Perhaps he had fallen asleep. It was difficult to tell. When he walked all night he would have a long siesta during the day. Sometimes he would not get up till six or seven in the evening. At other times he liked to talk as I drove. He talked about everything. In his slow hypnotic voice. The voice of an aristocrat, if you know what I mean, sir. But also the voice of someone who is not so much talking to you as talking to himself. When we die, Massimo, he said, we should make sure we do not leave chaos behind us. That would not be fair on those who come after us. No, he said, we should leave this life with everything in order. Everything should be labelled and classified. We will turn into dust, he said, but the music will live on. Music that is genuine will always live on, he said, just as music that is not genuine will soon wither and die, even if it brought fame and wealth to its composer in his lifetime. A true musician has a duty to his music, he said. If he believes in his music then he should believe that it will live on after his death.

— Was he happy that at the end of his life his works were at last being performed? I asked him.

— He did not say, he said.

— But you must have formed an impression.

— Since you ask me, sir, I have the impression that he was happy, he said. But also that he resented the time it took up that kept him away from his music. Monsieur Balise came to see me, he said. He was a waste of time, talking to me about Marmy and about mathematics. I had had enough of that sort of talk when I studied with Scheler in Vienna, he said. Scheler made me think, he said, and thinking is the worst thing a musician can do. It took me ten years to stop thinking after I left Vienna, he said. It was only Nepal that saved me from Vienna, he said. Scheler had studied with Schoenberg, he said, that is why I went to study with him. I have always wanted nothing but the best for my music, so I picked as a teacher a pupil of Schoenberg. What I had not grasped at the time was that Schoenberg, far from advancing the cause of music, as he claimed, had set music back a hundred years with his ideas and his theories and above all with his excessive Jewish anxiety. A composer cannot be anxious, Massimo, he said. To be anxious is to live in time, he said, and the composer does not live in time, he lives in eternity. When the composer understands that eternity and the moment are one and the same thing he is on his way to becoming a real composer, he said. Without that understanding he is nothing, He can be the most intelligent man in the world and the most profound, but he is not a composer. Schoenberg and Monsieur Balise were both highly intelligent, in some ways they were geniuses, he said. Their human ears were among the best the world has ever known, but they were merely human ears and for music you need an inner ear, *une oreille intérieure*, he said. Have you seen photographs of Stravinsky and Schoenberg Massimo, he said. Have you noticed the size of their ears? Do you think that is merely a coincidence? It is not a coincidence, he said, the size of their ears reflects their ability to discern human sounds. But the true composer does not listen to human sounds but to the sounds of the universe. Have you seen portraits of Bach and

Mozart? he said. Have you noticed their ears? I doubt if you have, he said, because the point about their ears is that they are unobtrusive ears. In other words they are normal human ears, a great deal smaller than yours, Massimo, though yours have no doubt been altered a little in the course of time by the blows life has inflicted on you. The ears of Bach and Mozart, on the other hand, he said, did not change much from their childhood to their death. They remained small, delicate, quite ordinary small and delicate ears. That is because they listened to inner and not to outer sounds. The inner ear, Massimo, that is what must be cultivated, the inner ear and the inner eye. Signor Berio came to see me, he said. He is a peasant. A man of the people. He has all the charm of the Italian peasant and all the limitations of that species. He is both innocent and cunning, he said, like the Italian peasant, who is incomparably superior to the French and the Spanish peasant, an incomparably superior human being and an incomparably superior tiller of the soil. But, he said, like the Italian peasant, Signor Berio is both lazy and self-satisfied. If he makes a beautiful sound and is paid a lot of money for doing so and the audience cheer and clap when the piece is performed he is satisfied. The curse of the age, Massimo, he said, is that people are too easily satisfied. They have forgotten how to listen with their inner ear, to listen to silence and to listen to the moment. Signor Berio justifies his large output by saying that he has to provide alimony for all his past wives, he said. Of course he says this as a joke, but there is a grain of truth in it. It never crosses his mind that he should not have married so many wives because, like the Italian peasant, he is at heart a sensualist. He feels that it is his right to sleep with a woman and to take his pleasure with her, it is his right that she should darn his socks and cook his meals. But it is not a right, Massimo, he said. That is why I have hired you, so that you can make sure I have a sufficient number of socks and that my shirts and ties and suits are always clean and freshly ironed. I pay you a great deal of money, Massimo, he said, and I pay Annamaria a great deal of money, but even so I pay less than Signor Berio spends on alimony to all his past wives. Monsieur Balise at least is not a sensualist, he said, but he is in the end what amounts to the same thing, he is an ascetic. He prides himself on living in hotels and out of a suitcase. He prides himself on having nothing to do with the bourgeois comforts of a family and a home. But he is in fact a living exemplar of what Ni Che described as the priestly spirit, the spirit of *ressentiment*. For he uses his asceticism as an instrument of power and he is not satisfied unless he has absolute power in the world of music. Signor Berio came to see me and drink wine with me in a spirit of peasant comradeliness, he said, and Monsieur Balise came to see me to exert his power over me. It all amounts to the same thing, he said. It all amounts to the negation of the spirit of music. Now I am famous, he said, and the world runs to my door, it expects me to throw that door wide open. But why should I do that? Why should I talk to these people and let them photograph my nose?

— Did he feel, I asked him, that hearing his own works played at last made a difference to his conception of them?

— No, sir, it made no difference, he said. He was very clear on that point. He said to me: When you are a real musician, Massimo, a real musician and hear with your inner and not your outer ear, then it makes no difference whether the works are performed or not. Of course, he said, it is of interest to hear

to undergo a rigorous training, not just a training in musicianship but a training in spirituality. The ears of the West cannot
tell the difference between a trumpet blown by a spiritual person
and a trumpet blown by a non-spiritual person, but the difference is everything, Massimo, he said, the difference is
everything.

– Did he speak to you about his visit to India and Nepal?

– He said: I only spent five months in India and Nepal. I
went with the expedition of the great Buddhologist Giuseppe
Tucci, he said, and they were the most important few months
of my life. I was interested in transcendence then, he said. There
are many roads to transcendence, he said. There is the way of
Indian mysticism, the way of Chinese mysticism, the way of
Nepalese and Tibetan Buddhism, the way of Sufism, the way
of Zen, the way of the Desert Fathers, the way of the Irish
monks, the way of St John of the Cross, and of course there is
the way of art. That is a very great way, Massimo, he said. *Une
grande voie. Une très grande voie.* When he was excited Mr Pavone
would lapse into French, one reason I believe why he liked
talking to me was because of the time I had spent in France and
my ability to understand the language. *Une très très grande voie,*
Massimo, he said. And music is the most direct of all the ways
of art, he said. It goes directly to the heart and directly to the
body. Music became too conscious at the beginning of the
twentieth century, he said, it was necessary to return it to its
roots in the unconscious. Some people call this inspiration, a
grand name for a simple thing. The root of the word inspiration is breath, he said, and all music is made of breath. If I have
given anything to music, he said, it is that I have given music
back its awareness of the importance of breathing, of breath.

Ruach, it is called in Hebrew, and with this *ruach* God created the world and with this *ruach* God created Adam, and it is this *ruach* that makes us live and also makes us spiritual beings.

He stopped. I waited for him to go on, but when it became clear that he was not going to, I said: Go on.

– I can't remember, he said.

– What can't you remember?

– Anything.

– Anything?

– What else he said about this.

– It doesn't matter. Talk about something else.

– Yes, sir, he said.

I waited.

Finally I said: Well?

– What would you like me to talk about, sir? he asked.

– What did he feel about living here in Rome?

– He said to me one day: Massimo, this is Rome. Rome is the boundary between East and West. South of Rome the East starts, and north of Rome is where the West starts. This border-line runs exactly over the Forum Romanum. This is where my house is, and this explains my life and my music.

– So he felt himself to be a Roman?

– He said to me: Massimo, I am a Sicilian, which means I am a stranger everywhere on earth. Sicily has rejected me, he said, and nowhere else has welcomed me as Dante, when he was exiled by his native city of Florence, was welcomed by Can Grande della Scala, the ruler of Ravenna. Fortunately, he said, I have always had enough money to live wherever I wanted. I lived in Monte Carlo when I was young and I was a popular figure at the balls and in the casinos and bridge clubs of the

Côte d'Azur. I lived in London after that and was a frequent visitor at the Court of St James. I lived in Vienna when I was studying with Scheler and frequented all the café-houses of the city. I lived in Switzerland during the war and got to know the sanatoria of that country better than anyone else, and the neurasthenics and madmen and lung cases who inhabited them. I lived in Paris after that and got to know the artists who at that time crawled all over the city. I was equally friendly with the tramps who slept by the Seine and with the Rothschilds in their grand houses on the *Isle* and in Neuilly. I have always loved extremes, he said. I am a man who is drawn to extremes. I can as easily wear a top hat at Ascot as a *béret basque* among the fishermen of Brittany or at the artists' ball in Montmartre. My biography, he said, could be written through the hats I have worn, the tennis caps in Monte Carlo and the pilgrim hats in Nepal, the grey top hats at Ascot and the black top hats for the premieres of Lord Berners' ballets, the colonial hats in the tropics and the Arab headdress in Egypt. Paris at the time, he said, was full of writers and poets. Pierre Jean Jouve, for instance. He was like the Eiger, like the north face of the Eiger. He had a head, I won't say like a pear, no, he had a head like a needle, a rock. No one else had such an intelligence, such sharpness. The way he spoke. And his translations of Shakespeare, such sharpness, such an instinct for the right word. Otherwise, intolerable, he said. An absolutely intolerable man. Only his wife could put up with him. His wife and all her patients. She had a large group of patients, because she was a psychoanalyst. Her patients were like a band of slaves. She made them run errands for her. She made them clean the house for her. She made them cook for her. In return she healed them. But they were all of them slaves. But Jouve had his good points, he said. The best was the fact that he got my poems published. He decided that my poems were worthy of being published. You can imagine, an Italian writing poetry in French. An Italian who has the temerity to write poetry in French. But he found some merit in them and he got them published. And there were many others, of course, before and after the war. Leiris. De Mondiargues. Soupault. Michaux was the one I was closest to, he said. Michaux was my closest friend, the closest thing I had to a friend. Michaux and his cat Ronaldo.

He stopped.

– Go on, I said.

– I cannot remember what was I saying, sir, he said.

– Michaux and his cat.

– Yes, thank you, sir. The trouble was, he said, I did not want to live in any of those places. I did not want to live in Monte Carlo or in London or in Vienna or in Switzerland or in Paris. I felt that the earth in those places rose up and rejected me. I tried to make a place for myself on this earth, he said. I married and had a beautiful house and entertained glamorous visitors. But all the time I felt the earth rising and pushing me away. Away, it said. Away. But away where? A man is born on this earth and if the earth rejects him where is he to go? To the moon perhaps? Or to Mars? But it will be the same there. The earth will rise up and reject you there because there is no longer a place for you in the universe. That is why I went to Nepal, he said. I am not a native of that region, and it would be foolish of me to imagine I could ever become one. But what my short trip to India and Nepal taught me is that it is possible to live with that rejection. You have to turn to your inner ear. You have to find a space within yourself. You have to make your music in that inner space. You have to furnish that inner space with enough furniture to live in a modicum of comfort. You have to have a table to eat off and a table to work at and a piano to work with and a bed to sleep in. You have to have a lavatory to shit in and a shower to wash under. Apart from that you need nothing. When I understood that, Massimo, he said to me, I was able to come home to my house here in Rome and settle down and work in peace. Until then I had been running round in circles, Massimo, he said. After that I was able to work in peace. Before that I had run after women and I had run after music and I had published poems and run after editors. After that I was able to sit at my piano and at my worktable in my house here in Rome and begin the work of my life. I do not regret the past, Massimo, he said. It is a mistake to regret the past because there is nothing we can do about it. It is the past and there is the end of it. If I had not run after women and music and all the rest of it perhaps I would never have been driven to join Tucci on his expedition to Nepal, he said. Perhaps I would never have been ready to listen to my inner ear. Once, he said, here in Rome, I met an old man. He was measuring some walls with a measuring rod. I was rather surprised since there are a lot of other devices to measure walls and distances with these days, as I said to him. There's nothing like handiwork, he said. I agreed with that. I said: I suppose you must know these walls and houses very well? As he turned I noticed that he had a small grey beard and very penetrating eyes. Yes, he said, I knew them before I started measuring them and now I don't know them any more. And then I realised he looked like Lao Tse.

— Like who?

— Lao Tse. Or something like that, sir.

— I see. And what did he say, this Lao Tse?

— That's all he said.

— That's all?

— Yes, sir. That's all Mr Pavone said he said, sir.

— I see. Go on.

— Yes, sir. How would you like me to go on?

— Go on with what you were saying.

— That's all. Mr Pavone didn't say anything more about him.

— Not subsequently?

— Not that I can remember, sir.

— I see. Tell me what your duties were in the house.

— Annamaria did the cooking and the washing. I looked after Mr Pavone's clothes and did other things like ordering his train and plane tickets and I ordered taxis for him when he needed them in Rome and of course I drove him when he wanted to be driven out into the Campagna.

— Who else did he employ?

— There was Annamaria and myself for the house. And, for his music, and to help him with the secretarial work and so on first he had Manfred Holthausen to do that. Then he had Yehuda Mazor. Then he had April Mauss. Then he had Alessandro Bonfiglioli. Finally, Sebastiano Testoro.

— Why so many?

— Mr Pavone had exacting standards, sir. He wanted his manuscripts just so. He told me: My scores are the record of my life. Some people write *War and Peace*, he said, I write *Akrita* and *Ruach*. Tolstoy's family preserved his manuscripts as holy relics. I do not have a family and I am not interested in holy relics, but I intend to leave all my manuscripts to the

Foundation I have set up, the Fondazione Tancredo Pavone, here in Rome, and I intend everything to be in order when I die. There is nothing more depressing, he said, than to try and bring order to the chaos left by the deceased. There is nothing more depressing than going through the wardrobes of the deceased and sorting out the clothes that should go to the family and those that can be given to charity and those that should be thrown away. There is nothing more depressing than sorting through trunkloads of old letters and papers in the vain hope that something of interest will turn up. No, he said. Everybody owes it to their executors to leave everything as well-organised as possible. I have kept all the letters sent to me in separate files under the names of the correspondents, he said, and these are arranged alphabetically in three large trunks in the attic, trunks to which I add periodically. I have had a catalogue made of all my books, he said, and designated which of them should remain in the Fondazione Tancredo Pavone and which should be sold and which should be given away. In all this, he said, Federico has been invaluable. He will be in charge of the Fondazione when I die. Order, he said. Order and hard work. Those are the keys. Of course, he said, without a radical reorientation of the self such as I underwent in Nepal, neither order nor hard work would be of any use at all. They would be a mockery, he said. An insult. But, given such a reorientation, only order and hard work will yield results. And if I work hard, he said, why should not those I pay to work for me work hard as well? He said that if they worked for him they should be dedicated to his music. If they are not dedicated to my music they are of no use to me, he said. If they are not dedicated to my music I might just as well employ a donkey, he said.

— He quarrelled with them?

— I would not say quarrelled. Mr Pavone was an aristocrat. He did not raise his voice. But if he felt they were not dedicated to his music he locked the door against them.

— Locked the door?

— At first they thought they had taken the wrong key, and they rang the bell, but when nobody answered they went away and telephoned. But I had instructions. When they came again and banged on the door I had to tell them that their service was terminated. I had to pack away their belongings and to give it to them without letting them into the house. That is when my size became an advantage. They asked to speak to Mr Pavone, of course, but he would not speak to them. Instead, he instructed me to tell them he had terminated their contracts. Of course this led to much abuse. But that was part of my job. They wrote him letters and Mr Holthausen even got his lawyers to write and threaten him, but he did not reply to their letters and nothing happened.

— But while they were working for him he treated them as friends?

— He was always correct with them.

— Meaning what?

— He was not a man who cared for intimacy.

— What kind of work did they do for him?

— I am not a musician. I cannot say.

— It has been said that they wrote the music he passed off as his own. What do you have to say to that?

— I am not a musician.

— But you know that he has been accused of making use of someone else's work.

— They have said that?

— It has been said.

— I wouldn't know, sir. I am not a musician.

— But he talked to you about his music.

— When we were driving. Late in his life. Then he would talk to me. About everything. About his childhood. About his marriage. About his friendships. Even about music. Really it was himself he talked to, sir, if you know what I mean. I was driving the car. He talked to me but I think he was really talking to himself.

— What did he say about his childhood?

— Oh, many things.

— Tell me some of the things.

— As you know, sir, he spent his childhood first in La Spezia, where his father, a naval officer, was stationed. But also in the family house in Sicily.

— What did he say about those years?

— He said that he began to improvise at the piano at the age of three. I would rush upon any piano that happened to be around, he said to me, and I would beat it with my fists and kick it with my feet. But no one ever said to me: What are you doing? You will break the piano. No. Everyone was astonished, but they never told me to stop, he said. I am eternally grateful to them for that. All through my life, he said, I have rushed upon everything, music and poetry, women and food, with my fists and my feet flailing out, but no one ever told me to hang back. It is to that I owe my musicianship, he said, which is better than that of anyone in the world because it is an uninhibited musicianship. Those composers who have learned how to write down notes and to compose complicated counterpoint and all the rest of it have been robbed of their patrimony, he said, which is the patrimony of hands and feet. *On les a privés de leur patrimoine, Massimo, he said, qui est le patrimoine des mains et des pieds.* We should attack everything in life as if it was a mortal enemy and a lover, as if it was both of those at once, a mortal enemy and a lover. Only Kleist understood this, he said, because he was an aristocrat and an officer. In the *Penthiselea* of Kleist, he said, which that old woman Goethe could not stomach because it gave him the shivers, the Amazon queen kills Achilles and then eats him because her love for him is too great for anything less, and in the end Kleist killed himself because his mouth was too small for the bites he wanted to take out of life. He killed himself, he said, in order to widen his mouth. If he had had the chance, as I had, to go to Nepal, he said, he would not have killed himself, he would have understood that there is an inner mouth which is bigger than any human mouth and that with that inner mouth we can bite off as much of the world as we want. My parents, he said, always let me do what I wanted. They did not try to send me to school or give me lessons of any sort which would have ruined my life before it had even begun, as it has ruined the lives of the majority of the civilised world, so called. In that way they laid the foundations for my music. Can anyone ask more of parents? he said. If I wanted to climb a tree, I climbed a tree. If I wanted to spend sixteen days and nights in the library, I spent sixteen days and nights in the library. They did this because my father was too busy with his naval duties and my mother was too busy with her dresses and her hair. Most of the time they forgot that I existed and it was only thanks to the servants that I survived. But that is better than being ordered about every hour of the day and made to do this and that and the other thing. Sometimes the serving girls took me into their beds and that is how I learned about women and sex, he said, without anxiety and without guilt, exactly in the way it should be. They made me realise that in addition to hands and feet we have sexual organs and that these sexual organs have been given us not only to reproduce but as a gateway to the feelings of the entire body, as the entrance way to pleasure. It would be better, he said, if those composers who live only to have their noses photographed for the papers had their sexual organs photographed instead, if instead of posing in front of the Forum and the Tower of Pisa and St Mark's in Venice and looking wise in their studies, they invited photographers into their bedrooms and bared their members. Then it would be obvious, he said, that there is absolutely no difference between a composer and a chimpanzee, except that a chimpanzee can scratch where a composer can't.

— Every child should be an only child, he said, there should be a law, as there is in China, against having more than one child. All the psychological harm inflicted on humanity, he said, has been inflicted not by fathers and mothers but by brothers and sisters. Freud never understood this, he said, obsessed as he was with fathers and mothers, but the truth is that it is brothers and sisters who do the most harm. In my time as an invalid in Swiss sanatoria, he said, I had the opportunity to observe the neurasthenic and the mad at close quarters, and you will not believe how often the cause of their illness was not a father or a mother but a brother or a sister. A child who has a brother or a sister can never be alone, and to be alone is the supreme joy of childhood as it is of adulthood. Give me the man who likes to be alone, Massimo, he said, and I will give you a happy and contented man. Every child should be allowed to develop as he wishes, he said. First, he said, I attacked every piano I came across with my fists and my feet. I banged the lids down and I caressed the strings and I used my elbows to smother the keys. The piano was my first love, he said. I found I could make it bring forth all the sounds I wanted and many that I had never dreamed of. It was lucky, he said, that the houses we lived in were so large, because even with all the doors shut I made an almighty din. I wanted nothing to do with the drawing-room sounds the piano brought forth when my parents invited the noted pianists and singers of the day to play and to sing, he said. I hated those pianists and those singers from the bottom of my heart. I hated the sounds they made and I hated the airs they gave themselves. It took two world wars to cleanse the world of such sounds and such airs, he said. And even today there are fools who invite pianists and singers into their homes to reproduce those sounds and those airs. They should be lined up against the walls of their drawing room and shot, he said, as should the pianists and singers they invite. The piano is a universe, Massimo, he said, it is not a world, it is not a country, and it is certainly not a drawing room, it is a universe. Observe the piano if you will, Massimo, he said, and see what it consists of. Look at the oddity of its shape and the variety of its surfaces. The piano is not an instrument for young ladies, Massimo, he said, it is an instrument for gorillas. Only a gorilla has the strength to attack a piano as it should be attacked, he said, only a gorilla has the uninhibited energy to challenge the piano as it should be challenged. It was when I realised this, he said, that I made a point of going to Africa to study the gorilla. When you see the chest and the brow of a gorilla, he said, you realise what a puny being man is. Liszt was a gorilla of the piano, he said. Scriabin was a gorilla of the piano. Rachmaninov was a gorilla of the piano. But the first and greatest gorilla of the piano was Beethoven, he said. Beethoven understood, he said, that the first attribute of the composer is deafness. All his life, he said Beethoven marched towards deafness as though towards his destiny. Between 1930 and 1945, he said, I wrote fourteen works for the piano, but by then I had been destroyed, first by Scheler in Vienna and then by my wife. It was only in 1951 that I returned to the piano, he said, and wrote seven works which came close to doing justice to the nature of the instrument. The culmination of this work was *Stepping into the Clouds* for four pianos, which was finished on 31 December 1955. Then I stopped. The piano no longer interested me. I still have my pianos, he said, and I still sometimes sit down at the piano, but I have exhausted the possibilities of the instrument. I have nothing more to say with it, he said, and it has nothing more to say to me.

— But he went on composing at the piano?

— At the piano?

— Yes.

— I do not understand the question.

— He had the piano by him when he was writing his music?

— There was always a piano in his study. But these are questions you will have to put to Mr Testoro. Only Mr Testoro was allowed into his study.

— Did Annamaria not go in to clean it?

— Nobody was allowed inside except Mr Testoro. Nobody is to go inside his study, Annamaria said to me. If you go inside his study that will be the end of you.

— So how was it cleaned?

– You will have to ask Annamaria.

– What were your relations with Mr Testoro?

– I do not think he ever had cause to complain about me.

– And the other secretaries?

– You will have to ask them.

– Is it true that Miss Mauss asked for you to be dismissed?

– You will have to ask her.

– That is what she has told me.

– That is her prerogative.

– You do not deny it?

– What would be the point of denying?

– But Mr Pavone did not dismiss you.

– That is correct.

– Instead, it was Miss Mauss herself who left?

– That is correct.

– Why did she leave?

– You will have to ask her yourself.

– Tell me about the house. How was it divided?

– It is a big house, as you know. The studio alone takes up two floors at the top and is the size of many fine flats here in Rome.

– Did you live on the premises?

– Yes. In the basement there were two flats. One for Annamaria and one for the help. And then, at the very top, above the studio, there is another flat, which Mr Pavone let to various people. Often to musicians who worked with him on his music. To performers.

– Who lived there in your time?

– For several years, when I first came, there was a quartet living there, who worked with Mr Pavone to perform his works for string quartet. He said to me: Anyone who performs my work, Massimo, must be like an extension of myself. They must become so used to playing my work that they can perform it in their sleep.

— They only played his work?

— They were hired by Mr Pavone to play his work. That was before many people were interested in his music. Before the Arditti Quartet took it up. It is fortunate, Massimo, he said, that I have money. My cousins want me to save my money so as to leave it to them and to their children when I die, but it is my money and I will do with it what I wish. If I had no money, he said, it would not be a tragedy. I would get by perfectly well. I have many skills, Massimo, he said, and I am not too proud to do any kind of work. But since I have money I will use it to further the cause of music and of civilisation.

— He said of music and civilisation?

— Those were his words, sir. To further the cause of music and of civilisation.

— Very good. Go on.

— In what direction, sir?

— In any direction you wish.

— I have forgotten what I was saying.

— Never mind. Tell me about the quartet. The performers.

— There was Mr Stankevitch. The quartet was named after him. The Stankevitch Quartet. And Mr Halliday. And Mr Silone. And Mr van Buren.

— Did you have much to do with them?

— No. They had the flat and they were quite independent.

— They spoke Italian?

— Yes. They all spoke Italian. Except Mr Halliday. Mr

Pavone spoke to them in French. Sometimes Mr Stankevitch and Mr van Buren spoke to each other in German. Or perhaps it was Czech or Dutch. And when they were all together they spoke in English.

— Did you ever hear them practising?

— No. As you know, sir, all the walls are soundproofed. Mr Pavone said to me: Massimo, there is nothing more exciting than the sounds of the street, but they should not enter the house. I have enough money, he said, to ensure that what goes on in one room of my house is not overheard in another room. There is nothing worse, he said, than hearing your neighbour playing his piano in what he thinks is a stylish way. It is worse even than hearing a radio or the senseless beat of a rock band on a record. Nothing worse, he said, than hearing the murmur of voices in a neighbouring room when you are trying to read or to think, let alone compose. Every room in this house is soundproofed, Massimo, he said. You could strangle your wife or your lover in your flat downstairs, Massimo, he said, and no one would be any the wiser. The Italians do not know what it means to be quiet, Massimo, he said. They are terrified of silence. I am not terrified of silence, he said. I crave silence as others crave drink. Of course, he said, scientists have shown us that there is no such thing as perfect silence. In the best sound-proofed room in the world you will hear the blood roaring in your veins and your heart beating against your ribs. But it is your blood, Massimo, he said, and your heart. That is the difference, he said.

He was silent.

I waited.

After a while I said: Go on.

– Yes, sir, he said.

– Did Mr Pavone say anything more about silence? I asked him.

– I can't remember, he said.

– All right, I said. Tell me: were the quartet already there when you arrived?

– Yes, sir.

– And they never talked to you?

– Sometimes Mr Silone would stop on the stairs and we would have a chat.

– What about?

– Many things.

– Like what?

– Many things.

What sort of things?

– Often about football. We were both supporters of Lazio.

– I see. And why did they eventually leave?

– I think Mr Pavone no longer required them.

– It is not that they quarrelled?

– I could not say, sir. He said to me: One day there will be a quartet that will be able to play my music for string quartet. By then I will be long dead. *Je serai mort depuis longtemps*, Massimo, he said.

– He often spoke to you in French?

– When there was something he had been thinking about for a long time he often said it in Italian first and then in French. French was once the language of the aristocracy, he said to me. From Moscow to Paris the aristocracy of Europe spoke in French. It was the *lingua franca*, Massimo, he said to me. Now that there is no longer an aristocracy everybody speaks in

English, the language of money. English is not a language, Massimo, he said to me, it is a hybrid. It is made up of a bit of Latin and a bit of Celtic and a bit of German and a little bit of Norse and some French and a little bit of Hindi and Arabic and Dutch and much else besides.

– Who else occupied the flat in your time with Mr Pavone?

– After the quartet, a cellist. A lady. Very correct.

– Did Mr Pavone entertain at all?

– No. He said to me: When I was young, Massimo, I thought music and social life could mix, but after a certain age you realise that music is music and life is life.

– So he lived a solitary existence?

– Occasionally he would go out to dinner with friends. I would order a taxi for him and give the driver the address. Mr Pavone had many friends among the aristocracy and in the film and theatre world. I would rather speak to a landowner who wishes to talk only about his pigs and his olive trees, or even to a self-satisfied and pompous actor, than to a musician, he said. I do not need musicians, Massimo, he said to me. I have quite enough of them in my bathroom when I look in the mirror. When I go out, he said, it is to escape from music and musicians, not to subject myself to their vanity and paranoia. The vanity and paranoia of musicians, Massimo, he said to me, is beyond belief. Each of them thinks he is the centre of the universe, he said, each of them thinks that if only the world was prepared to listen to his music all its problems would be solved. Each of them thinks his colleagues and rivals are worth nothing and less than nothing and take up space which he would better fill himself. My wife, he said, thought of herself as a generous person, she thought of herself as an understanding person, but she was neither generous nor understanding. The only person she understood was herself and her needs.

— He was in love with his wife?

— I do not know. He said to me once: When you are young you meet a beautiful woman and want to sleep with her and so you persuade yourself that you are in love with her. But you are not in love with her. You are in love with yourself and your possibilities. And she is in love with herself and her own possibilities. The two are quite different, Massimo, he said. If my wife had not left me in 1945, he said, I would still be married to her today and I would have done absolutely nothing with my life. When she left me, he said, I wanted to kill myself. I had lost my way in music and I had lost my way in love. When she left me I had to start all over again from the beginning.

— And what became of her?

— He did not say. He only talked of her leaving him. When a woman you love leaves you, Massimo, he said, it is as though the world itself had left you. For a while you feel as though there is no world left for you to live in. When she left me, he said, I couldn't go into my study, I couldn't look at my scores. I was afraid to go out and I was afraid to stay at home. Afraid of what? Of my thoughts. Of the intensity of my feelings for her. Everything I did and everything I had done disgusted me. If I had not gone to Nepal in 1949 I would have been dead within a year, he said. Instead, I was reborn.

— He said that? Instead, I was reborn?

— I think so, yes.

— You cannot remember exactly?

— Yes. He said that.

— What did he say about that time?

— He said he was afraid to go out.

— Yes. You told me that.

— Yes, sir.

— How did they meet?

— It was when he was in England, as a young man, at the Court of St James, he said.

— What is the Court of St James?

— I do not know, sir.

— All right. Go on.

— When I had had enough of Monte Carlo, he said, I decided to go to England, to spend a little time in London, he said. I had an introduction to the English composer Lord Berners, he said, and through him I met the cream of the English aristocracy.

— What did he mean, the cream of the English aristocracy?

— I do not know.

— All right. Go on.

— I met the cream of the English aristocracy, he said. You must understand, Massimo, he said, that the European aristocracy is all interrelated, but that a German aristocrat is very different from a French aristocrat and a French aristocrat is very different from an English aristocrat. The French aristocracy was largely destroyed by the French Revolution, he said, and in its place a new aristocracy was created which is not an aristocracy at all but a jumped-up bourgeoisie which gives itself airs. Lord Berners, he said, could trace his family back to the Norman Conquest. He was a man after my own heart. He was a man who did not give a fig for what other people thought. It is a pity, he said, that he was not a serious composer, but then the English have never been serious about anything. That is their charm but also their weakness. There is only one thing the English care about, and that is money, he said. But not the aristocracy. Since they have money they are not interested in it. Lord Berners was an accomplished comic writer, he said, a better writer than Ronald Firbank, in my view, but as a composer he was a lightweight. The English have not had a major composer since Purcell, he said, and to think they once led the way in the art of composition. To think that they once produced the likes of Dunstable and Byrd and Tallis, to say nothing of Dowland and of the anonymous composers of the Eton Choirbook and the Old Hall Manuscript. They have been ruined by the Industrial Revolution, he said, and by the spirit of Protestantism. Also by the Germanic cast of their minds. They have an indigestible cake, he said, called a lardy cake, and their leading modern composers, so-called, Sir Edward Elgar and Sir Ralph Vaughan Williams, are the musical equivalents of this cake. Even when you get a refined musician like Benjamin Britten, he said, he cannot escape the terrible English sentimentality when he composes, though that is blessedly absent when he plays the piano, which he does to very good effect. He is not a gorilla of the piano, but he is, let us say, a gazelle of the piano, and that is no mean thing.

He stopped.

I waited for him to go on. When he showed no sign of doing so I said: Go on.

— Yes, sir, he said.

— What did he say about his years in Vienna? I asked him.

— He said: After I had been in England for several years I decided to pursue my musical interests in a more rigorous fashion. So I went to Vienna to study with Schoenberg and his pupils and I was taken on by Walter Scheler. My friends were amazed that I had been able to attach myself to Scheler, he said, but I was only interested in the best. However, he said, although I studied with Scheler for barely two years, it took me at least ten years to get over it.

— What did he mean by that?

— There must be a reason for every note, Scheler said, Mr Pavone told me, but he never asked himself what a note was. Like all the musicians of Vienna he thought of himself as a radical but he would never let you question the fundamentals of composition. For them a note was a part of a structure, what a note was *in itself*, what a sound was *in itself*, that was never questioned.

— Was he living alone in Vienna?

— Yes. He said to me: London was where I experimented with women and Vienna was where I experimented with notes.

— Did he not meet his wife in London?

— Yes.

— But he did not take her to Vienna with him?

— She did not want him in London. She ran away from him and when he followed her and brought her back she ran away again. He said to me: When you are young you think that when a woman refuses you she is simply being coy. It never strikes you that she might not like you or be interested in you. When you are young, he said, your narcissism is so great you imagine you are irresistible. I had had enough of women in London, he said, I had had enough of them in Italy and in Monte Carlo and in London, and I went to Vienna to get to the root of my musical impulses. But in Vienna they almost killed me with thought. Thought, he said, is the great enemy of the artist, but in Vienna they wanted you to think your way through every difficulty. One cannot think one's way through artistic problems, he said, one has to go about it in a different way. Bach did not think, he said, he danced. Mozart did not think, he sang. Stravinsky did not think, he prayed. But in Vienna they had forgotten how to dance, they had forgotten how to sing, they were all secular Jews and they had forgotten how to pray. Schoenberg was a real musician, he said, but he was a disaster for music. Schoenberg, he said, set Western music back by fifty years, if not a hundred. He terrified his pupils and stopped them thinking for themselves. Had they thought for themselves they would have understood that thought is a disaster for music. It took me ten years to recover from Scheler, he said, and there were times when I thought I would never do so. Had I not gone to Nepal when I did, he said, I doubt if I would ever have recovered from Scheler and Schoenberg and Vienna. In Vienna, he said, I couldn't look at a score without thinking. I couldn't strike a note on the piano without thinking. I had ceased to listen and I had ceased to want to make, the two essential prerequisites for the composer. I knew only one thing, that I had to think and account for every note. But why should the sequence of notes be the essence of music? I had known that it was not from the age of three, from the time when I began to attack the piano with my hands and feet. I had known it every time I saw a lovely woman or passed my hand over her breast or buttock. I had known it, you could say, from the moment I was born. But that wretched Scheler almost made me forget it. That is what education does for you, he said, it draws you along paths you know are not real paths until you forget that they are not real paths and think they are the only paths. When I went to Nepal, he

said, and I first heard the temple bells and the temple gongs and
the temple trumpets, it brought back to me what I had known
from the day I was born, but which Schoenberg and Scheler and
Vienna had made me forget, that it is not a question of notes,
it is a question of attitude. The church bells of Europe have
long ceased to make music, he said, they jingle like a music box
but they do not make music. But the bells and gongs and trumpets of the Buddhist temples of Nepal and Tibet bring you back
to the roots of music. Each sound I heard, Massimo, he said,
had taken a lifetime to produce, what do I say, many lifetimes,
many generations, to produce, and I realised that each sound is
a world, an infinite world, Massimo, it is like a huge cavern
which can take a lifetime to explore and yet which is over in no
time at all, it is almost as if you could say that it does not exist
in time at all. That was the mystery and the paradox I had to
grapple with when I returned to Rome, he said, when I returned
to my empty house here on the *Foro*, that was the paradox I
began to explore in the first works I would truly claim as my
own, *Hun dun* for solo oboe, *Only by Bending* for bass clarinet,
and, above all *Écluse* for chamber ensemble. That was the first
phase of my career, he said, eight magical years in which single-
handedly I rethought the possibilities of music. The climax of
that period, he said, was the imaginary puppet opera, *Can You
Be a Baby Boy?* which was performed here in the house by the
very best singers and musicians that money can buy, which I
had performed for myself and a few friends. Michaux came
from Paris, he said. And so did Leiris. Pasolini came. Maraini,
who had been to Nepal with me. A few others. After that I
stopped composing for two years, I thought my task in the
world was done.

He stopped.

— Go on, I said.

— That's what Mr Pavone said: I thought my task in the world was done.

— And then?

— Then he was silent.

— I mean at other times.

— About his music?

— Yes.

— Once he said to me: Massimo, I am going to tell you a story. Once upon a time, he said, there was a Zen master. His pupil said to him: What can I do to save me from distraction? He said to his pupil: You must listen to the world. His pupil said to him: How can I listen to the world? You must listen to the beating of the heart of the flea, the master said. How can I do that? asked the pupil. Take a flea, the master said, and then stretch a piece of string about a two elbows' length and tie it to two stakes which you will stick in the ground, about three elbows' length from the ground. A flea is a very high jumper, Massimo, he said to me, but if you put a flea on a piece of string it does not jump off. So you put the flea on the string and lie down beneath it, looking up at it. The flea will walk the length of the string first one way and then the other, without stopping, he said. At first, the master said to his disciple, all you will see, by staring really hard, is this tiny flea walking along the string one way and then back and then one way again and then back. But after a day of this, he said to his disciple, you will begin to see the flea swelling, and after three days and nights of watching, it will be so big you will be able to see its heart beating, beating, beating in its breast, and you will hear the beating as a roar of thunder and the heart will grow as big as a house and you will want to put your fingers to your ears and to close your eyes because the noise will be so loud, the noise of the flea's heart beating, and the flea will be so huge. At that point, the master said to his disciple, you will know what it means to see the beating of a flea's heart. And after that you will be able to see the world as it asks to be seen and to listen to each sound as it asks to be listened to. That is what I have tried to do, Mr Pavone said to me. I have tried to make people listen to each beating of the heart of the flea.

He stopped.

— Go on, I said.

— Yes, sir, he said.

— What else did he say about his music?

— He said to me once: The life of the composer is a solitary life, but it is the best life there is. A composer, he said, who has the time to do what he does best, that is, compose, is the happiest being alive. To be creative, Massimo, he said to me, is to be in a state of constant openness to the world. That does not mean that there are not dark moments, Massimo, he said, there are and there always will be, but they are part of the whole and must be seen as such. To be open, Massimo, he said, does not mean to be driven, as Schoenberg was driven, it does not mean working at your desk for sixteen hours every day, it means being like a flower, Massimo, he said, a human flower. John Cage, he said to me, was a person after my own heart. He understood what it means to be open to the world. Unfortunately what talent he had in his youth had been eradicated by his theories. John Cage had theories about everything, he said, but especially he had theories about not having theories. That is

very American, Massimo, he said. You find it in Whitman. You
find it in Pollock. And I found it in Cage. The Americans want
to invent the wheel afresh each time they draw breath. They are
sublimely innocent, he said, which helps them to make money
but is a disaster for their artists. John Cage's instincts were all
good, he said, but he was too much influenced by Marcel
Duchamp and by Dada. Dada was good for the First World
War, he said, but it was no good at all for 1950. I knew many
of the Surrealists, Massimo, he said to me. I met them in Paris
both before and after the war. Michel Leiris. Philippe Soupault.
André Pieyre de Mondiargues. Breton himself. Dali. Jouve.
They were all interesting men. Soupault was an anthropologist.
He had travelled in Africa and worked in Mexico. Leiris too.
But they were in thrall to a pernicious ideology. They recognised that reason is both limited and limiting, but they imagined
that the opposite of reason was the unconscious. Dreams.
Nonsense. They did not understand that you have to go down
a long and difficult road if you are to leave reason behind. You
cannot do it overnight. That is why their works feel like
schoolboy pranks. Michaux was different, he said. Michaux was
a good friend of mine, he said. His art and his poetry came from
the heart. Lutosłavski set Michaux's great poem about the
wrestling match between two giants, 'Le Grand Combat', not for
single voice but for large choir. That was a stroke of genius. It
is his best work, but the recording is lousy. It set a new low in
the recording of contemporary music. I played chess with Marcel
Duchamp, he said. I thought I was quite a proficient chess
player, but he was on another plane. As a chess player he was on
another plane. *A un tout autre niveau.* And perhaps as an artist as
well. He was on another plane from the Surrealists and the

Dadaists. But nobody built on his legacy. They couldn't, because his legacy was quicksand. Only Charles Ives and Edgar Varèse have known what it is to be a composer in America, he said. Apart from popular geniuses like Gershwin and Berlin, who managed to marry the bittersweet sadness and nostalgia of East European Jewish music with the nostalgia of Black American music. Song in the hands of Gershwin and Berlin became what it had always been in European music, he said, a vehicle for the body to express itself. The language of music is not the sonata and it is not the tone row, he said, it is the same kind of language as weeping, sobbing, shrieking and laughing. That is why music has always been seen as the medium of communication with the spirit world. But the modern world has forgotten this, he said. The sophisticated composers of the modern world have forgotten it. They have been haunted by the idea of opera, he said, but because they have forgotten the bodily origins of music it has nearly always proved to be a disastrous lure for them.

— What did he mean, a disastrous lure?

— That is the phrase he used. A disastrous lure. We were driving to Palestrina one spring day. He had told me the story of Lord Berners and his trips into the Campagna in his big car and he said —

— What story of Lord Berners?

— Lord Berners, Mr Pavone said, lived in Rome and Naples for a while. He had a harpsichord installed in the back of his Rolls and while his chauffeur drove through the quiet countryside of the Campagna he would put on one of the African masks he had acquired and play the music of Pergolesi and Bach, of Couperin and Rameau, especially the very fast music of these composers, on the harpischord in the back of the car. They would drive through peaceful villages which had never seen a car before, never mind a car with a harpsichord in the back being played by a man in an African mask, and the villagers would cross themselves and go back into their houses. The harpsichord had been specially built to go into his car, Mr Pavone said, and —

— Never mind Lord Berners. You were talking about the phrase 'a disastrous lure', I reminded him.

— You asked me what story, he said.

— All right, I said. Go on.

He was silent.

— Go on, I said.

— I can't remember, he said, hanging his head.

— The idea of opera, I encouraged him.

— Ah yes, he said. The idea of opera. Opera, Massimo, he said to me, is the will o' the wisp that has lured the modern composer to his doom. Because composers in the past wrote operas these people think that this is what they still have to do. But what they do not understand, Massimo, he said, is that there is such a thing as a cultural imperative. A cultural imperative, Massimo, he said. The cultural imperative of the Renaissance led to the composition of the mass; the cultural imperative of the Baroque led to the composition of oratorio. That is because these were still cohesive societies. The cultural imperative of Romanticism led to the concerto, to lieder, and to Romantic opera, the solitary lament of the solitary self. Romantic opera, he said, is entertainment for the masses, for the solitary individuals who make up the masses. It is dressed up as passion, the passion of desire, the passion of love and the losing of love, for which the only remedy is death. But that is only dressing up, Massimo, he said, only camouflage. What it is really about is the loss of society. That is what these operas really lament, he said, the loss of the spirit of society which inspired the masses and oratorios of the past. Modern opera, he said, either tries to pretend that the old forms are still viable, or it tries to reinvent the form. Perhaps in the future someone will come who will reinvent opera altogether, but for the moment it is impossible. Serious composers will always come to grief with opera today, he said as we were driving to Palestrina, no matter how they set about their task, whether, like Henze and Britten, by trying to breathe life into moribund forms, or, like Nono, by getting his architect friends to build him a special box for his opera and his intellectual friends to write him incomprehensible texts for his opera, texts made up of Greek and German, because for Italians, Massimo, he said, to be able to refer to Greek and German mythology and especially to be able to quote in the original Greek and German, shows that you are a cultured man, shows that you have finally left the hovel of the peasant and entered the city of Culture. All a disaster, he said. Henze a disaster. Britten a disaster. Dallapiccola a disaster. Nono a disaster. Berio a disaster. Bussotti a disaster. Have you noticed, by the way, Massimo, he said, how many composers have names starting with the letter B? To get a comprehensive knowledge of Western music, he said, you need only listen to works by composers whose names begin with B. That is itself a reason, he said, if your name does not begin with B, for wishing to escape from that tradition. Do you know why all these modern composers want to write operas? he said. It is because they feel they have suffered too much, hidden away in their rooms writing music, and now they want to come up onto the stage like Caruso and Pavarotti and take their bow and have lovely ladies swoon at their feet at the reception afterwards and invite them back to their beds. They feel they have paid their dues to the Muses in all the years of work in closed rooms by themselves with no lovely ladies interested in them and no fame and no money and so now they feel they are owed all this by society and by so feeling they give notice of their essentially *petit bourgeois* mentality and of their essential triviality. I had had my fill of wealth and fame and pretty ladies by the time I left Monte Carlo in 1927, he said, and I was only twenty-two, but these are men of fifty and sixty and they feel that their lives have not yet begun, so they write operas in order to be able to put down their pencils at last and jump into bed with pretty ladies who are not their wives, and of course some of them even manage to do that.

— What did he say about Monte Carlo?

— He said to me: At sixteen, Massimo, I had had enough of being a child. I had had an old-fashioned education of Latin, chess and fencing, and been given plenty of free time to develop my interests, I had learned all the essentials of sex from my cousin Lara and from the serving-girls, but now I wanted to stretch my wings. He said that he went to stay with a cousin of his in Monte Carlo and there he learned to play bridge and to gamble in the casino and to dance. Monte Carlo at the time, he said, was the haunt of the most elegant men in the world. Theo Rossi di Montelera was commonly regarded as the most elegant, he said, but to my mind a Frenchman, Guy de la Lagardière was even more elegant. The most elegant of all, however, was Prince Yusupof, who was said to have organised the murder of Rasputin. His was not so much a sartorial elegance, as an elegance of posture and movement. It was not the elegance of Fred Astaire, no, that was something quite different. Yusupof,

he said, made one think of those long-haired Russian grey-
hounds whose every step evokes a spontaneous beauty and an
unsurpassable elegance. It was in Monte Carlo, he said, that I
found I had a talent for dancing, he told me, and also for writing
waltzes and other dances of the time. I was soon in demand as
a partner for many beautiful women, he said, and hostesses
began to ask me to compose music for the bands that played at
their houses. I sometimes played the piano at these soirées, he
said, and partnered some of the older ladies at bridge. I seem to
have needed very little sleep in those days, he said, because when
the night was done and the others went home to their beds I
stayed at the piano and wrote my music, and even when I went
to bed, he said, it was rarely by myself, and as you know,
Massimo, there is nothing less conducive to sleep than sharing
your bed with someone. Soon, he said, I abandoned my cousin,
much to his annoyance, and found a flat of my own, a beautiful
flat, like all the flats of Monte Carlo, with a beautiful view of
the sea and the mountains. I should have learned from that time,
Massimo, he said to me as we were driving one day, after he had
had his first stroke, I should have learned that the secret of
writing music is not thinking but feeling happy and feeling full.
When you are full of the smells and sounds of the world, he
said, when you are full of passion for a beautiful woman, music
is an overflow, and that is a guarantee of authenticity. What I
wrote then was not worth a bean, he said, and no one ever imagined it was, but it had a natural quality which I then lost for
thirty years and only rediscovered on my return from Nepal in
1949. This is a quality which cannot be learned, Massimo, he
said, it is there or it is not there. When I subsequently went on
my ethnographical trips to West Africa, he said, I immediately

sensed that the most striking quality of the art I found there was not its abstraction or its primitiveness or even its beauty, but its authenticity: you had the feeling that it had to be like this and no other way. When I went to the territory of the Ife with Daniel Bernstein, who had been a pupil of Frobenius, he said, I felt that I had entered a world of which I had often dreamed but which Europe had been unable to provide for me. The bronze heads of the Ife and of course of the Benin region are now famous the world over, he said, but in those days they were only just beginning to be known. Frobenius was so struck by what he took to be the classicism of these heads, he said, that he posited a historical link with ancient Greece, ridiculous of course, the Ife and Benin heads have a warmth and a humanity, a grace and a graciousness that is quite missing from classical Greek heads. The most remarkable sculptures of the Ife, though, he said, the memory of which has never left me in the course of my life, are the stone sculptures found in the groves or religious sanctuaries that are dotted about the periphery of the city of Ife. There are remarkable standing figures, such as the one called the Gatekeeper, a hideous dwarfish creature who guards one of the groves and to whom the people still brought offerings when I was last there in 1932 and perhaps they still do today. But for me, he said, in the first expedition I undertook with my dear friend Daniel Bernstein in 1926, for me the most overwhelming object was a granite slab some two metres high by forty centimetres broad and about ten centimetres thick, with five holes drilled into its upper half, and which ethnologists have called the Shield. Why that should have made such an impression on me is difficult to understand, he said, but I felt the moment I saw it as though I was standing at the confluence of all the waters of the world, I felt an immense pressure on all sides, which was keeping me upright and keeping me stable, but only because the pressure was so evenly distributed. I have often thought of that moment, he said, I felt it again when I heard the great trumpets being sounded during my trip to Nepal, and of course I have felt it when composing the music I have written since that time. You feel, he said, as if at every moment you are going either to be crushed or swept away, but you also feel as if you are in touch with the secret pulse of the universe. It is an extraordinary sensation, he said, a compressing into the moment of everything that has ever been and ever will be. It is this that I look for in each sound I imagine, he said, it is this that is at the heart of every note.

I waited for him to go on, but when he remained silent I said: Go on.

— No, he said.

— You are tired? I asked him.

— No, he said.

— If you are tired we can take a break.

— No, I am not tired, he said.

— Then why do you not go on?

— I am remembering Mr Pavone, he said.

— Remembering what about him?

— Just remembering him.

I waited a while. Then I asked him again: Shall we take a break?

— No, he said.

I waited.

— In a minute I will go on, he said.

I waited again. Then I said: How did he meet Mr Bernstein?

— He met him in Monte Carlo, he said. The four years he spent there, Mr Pavone told me, from the ages of sixteen to twenty, were among the happiest of his life. I was young, he said. I was handsome. I was rich. I was talented and I was care-free. I spent my days playing tennis and sailing and swimming, and my nights dancing with beautiful women. What more can one ask for at that age? I was as happy as I would ever be, but at the same time I already understood that happiness is not enough. The human being who no longer needs to spend his days hunting for food, he said, or to spend his days earning enough to pay for the food he needs, wants something more in his life than happiness. Or perhaps it was me, he said, for my cousin Tarquinio did not seem to be driven by the same need. Tarquinio believed that there was no reason why the life he was living in Monte Carlo should not last for ever. In Rome, he said to me, that idiot Mussolini is trying to whip the Italian people into hysteria, but here in Monte Carlo we can ignore him and his rallies, we can live as God meant us to live. By this he meant eating as much as he could and sleeping with as many beautiful women as he could, without taking any thought for the fact that these two things do not run in parallel lines and that while a well-fed youth might appeal to women, especially if he has a lot of money, an obese middle-aged man, even if wealthy, would appeal only to the kind of woman he would not really want to be with. As for me, he said, there was never any danger that I would grow obese, partly because neither of my parents is obese, and partly because I danced so much and played so much tennis and went for such long hikes in the Alps that I was unlikely to put on any weight, no matter how much I ate, and I have never been a big eater. Writing music and sleeping with beautiful women and, when I was young, dancing and playing tennis, those were the things I was passionate about, not eating or sleeping. I have never needed much food or much sleep, he said, which is a blessing, because some of my best musical ideas have come at night when walking through the streets of Rome. Cities, he said, should be walked through at night, that is when you become aware of the soul of a city, and Rome is the quintessential city. The conversations you have in a city at night, with passing strangers and the people you meet in all-night bars far surpass the conversations you have during the day. During the day everyone is busy, everyone is going about his or her business, he said, but at night it is as though the notion of ends disappears and each moment is valued in and for itself. Everyone who walks through a city at night walks in the present, he said, while everyone who walks through a city during the day walks in the past or the future. The very buildings of a city seem to return with a sigh to the present moment when night falls, he said, especially if there is a full moon. Nowadays, when the howl of police sirens destroys the calm, it is sometimes difficult to remain in the present, even at night. Police sirens cannot help but remind you of the past and the future, cannot help tearing you away from the present. Varèse, who was a very great composer, he said, imagined that he was being modern by introducing a police siren into his works, but all that did was date his works and limit their interest. It is quite incredible, he said, how many artists have been ruined by half-baked ideas about what will make them modern. Varèse was one of the most uncompromising composers who ever lived, he said, and yet his works are frequently ruined by naive ideas about what it means to be modern. That can never be said of Stravinsky, he said. I stole shamelessly from Stravinsky, he said, in the fourteenth of my *Canti*. For the vocal part I borrowed directly from Stravinsky's writing for the voice in *Les Noces*, arguably the greatest work he ever wrote. But then Stravinsky stole shamelessly from Pergolesi and from Handel and from many others. It is only timid souls who are afraid to steal. Henri Michaux, he said, whom I got to know when I was living in Paris in the years before and after the war, said to me one day: All artists are cannibals, and the bigger the artist the bigger the cannibal. Michaux it was who encouraged me to write poetry in French. It is always important to try one's hand at different arts, Michaux said. I am a writer but I also draw and paint. Why? Because there is an immediacy about drawing and painting that you cannot get when you use words. Words and sentences have been used since time immemorial, he said, but when I put my pencil on the page I can let it roam where it will, I can let it surprise me, I can let it do things no one has ever done before. Perhaps, he said, you are driven to write poetry as well as to compose for a reason you do not understand yourself. But if you are driven then you should let yourself go. Michaux encouraged me and Jouve found me a publisher, he said.

– Did he ever recite his own poetry to you?

– No, sir, not that I can remember.

– Did he talk much about it?

– No, sir.

– Did he not think of himself as a poet as well as a composer?

– I do not know, sir.

– Did you get the impression when you knew him that he still wrote poetry?

– No, sir.

— He thought of himself only as a composer?

— He did not think of himself as a composer, sir. More as a conduit for sound. If anyone ever calls me *maestro* in your hearing, Massimo, he said to me, I give you full permission to take that person by the scruff of the neck and show them the door. Here in Italy, he said, as well as in France and Germany, the culture of authority and deference has never gone away. Just as a courtier, Massimo, he said to me one day as we drove to Orvieto, just as a courtier hopes to get in his master's good books by calling him Sire and Your Majesty all the time, so these little mini-courtiers who haunt the corridors of the concert halls and opera houses think you will grant them favours if they call you *maestro*. A cook is a *maestro*, Massimo, he said to me. A conductor is a *maestro*. But is a composer a master? What is he a master of? The art of composition, Massimo, he said to me, is the art of submitting, not of mastering, it is the art of listening, not of speaking, it is the art of letting go, not of holding on. In this house, Massimo, he said, I am the master because I pay the wages, but at my desk what am I? Nothing. That devil Scheler tried to make a master out of me in Vienna, he said. He tried to make me master the art of composition, as he put it. He wanted me to be able to explain to him why every note was where it was and not in some other place. He wanted me to master the notes, to become a little *Meistersinger* of Vienna. But I could not master the notes. Even then I felt it was the notes that were mastering me. It was a cold day in early April. He wanted to go to Orvieto to study the images on the columns of the cathedral there. Those columns are among the wonders of the world, Massimo, he said to me, and no one goes to see them, while everyone goes to gawp at the grotesque homoeroticism of Michelangelo's ceiling in the Sistine Chapel. And why do they do that? Only because they have been told it is a masterpiece. Do they know what a masterpiece is? Do they realise that works of art are no more masterpieces than your mother, Massimo, is a masterpiece? No. Sheep, Massimo, sheep, he said. Sheep without the innocence of sheep. Sheep without the kindly disposition of sheep. That is the kind of sheep they are, Massimo, he said to me. How many people does one meet in one's life who do anything other than follow the leader? Three, he said. I perhaps met three in my lifetime. There was Daniel Bernstein, with whom I went to West Africa and to Egypt. There was Henry Michaux. And there is Matthaeus, whom I see occasionally here in Rome, a man of independent spirit and independent mind. That is all, he said. Three in seventy years. Less than one for every twenty years. What does that say about the human race, Massimo, he said, what does that tell us about our brothers and sisters, so-called? But it has always been like that, he said. Nothing new. When you look back at the history of the world, Massimo, he said to me, what you see is the history of sheep. Of madmen leading sheep and sheep following madmen. Nothing else. I at least can say that I have not been a sheep, Massimo, he said. And that I owe largely to my parents, who gave me the opportunity to develop the way I wanted and to find out what my true path was. And to my chance meeting with Daniel Bernstein in Switzerland, he said. To our chance meeting on the top of a mountain, when I was at an impressionable age. Our trip to West Africa in 1925, he said, was the making of me. To be in the presence of a man like Daniel, he said, was to learn what it means to be a free spirit. He made us leave the car at the bottom of the hill and walk up to the cathedral. The motorcar is a wonderful invention, Massimo, he said, but we must make the effort to approach a building such as a cathedral in the right spirit. I understood the nature of our patrimony, Massimo, he said, when I was shown round the temples of India and Nepal. There I observed a relationship to the space of the building on the part of the worshippers that was once the norm in Europe but has since been forgotten. A temple or a cathedral, Massimo, he said to me, is more than the building you see before you. It is the centre of a sacred space which spreads far beyond the precincts of the temple or the cathedral as such. The approach to such a space is itself a rich experience, he said, for it is the approach to a presence, the presence of the saint or holy man towards whom you are travelling. Even today, he said, when they fill our churches and cathedrals with ghastly so-called religious music beamed out of invisible loudspeakers, even today these buildings have a power over us. Varèse always said that to understand his music you had to understand that he had grown up in the shadow of that great building, the Abbey of Tournus. I myself am fortunate that I only grew up in the vicinity of the little chapel that formed part of our property and that my free-thinking parents treated it as a likeable anachronism. Churches are a wonder, Massimo, he said, but the Church is an unmitigated disaster, as are all large bureaucracies, whether it be those of the ancient Egyptians or the Aztecs or the Soviets or any other empire. It is they who foster the spirit of subservience, it is they who turn us all into sheep. But they cannot be blamed for everything, because after all it is the sheep who instituted the empires and the bureaucracies. In the Book of Samuel, Massimo, he said to me, which as a good Catholic you have never read, in the Book of Samuel the prophet Samuel pleads with the Israelites not to choose a king to rule over them, but they are sheep, Massimo, he said, they are sheep and they want to be like other sheep. Give us a king, they say. Give us a king. And they will not rest till they have one. That is what these Zionists want to set up again, Daniel said to me as we walked round the sacred groves of Ife, they are tired of living without a king and country of their own, which is what has made them what they are, and now they want a country and a bureaucracy and a military and all the other trappings of nationhood. The sacred groves of Ife, he said, were just about as far as one could get from the ballrooms and casinos of Monte Carlo, but for a while in the 20s I moved happily between them. When I was dancing and gambling and playing bridge and tennis in Monte Carlo, he said, I was longing for the sacred groves of Ife, and when I was in West Africa what kept me going in the heat and the endless rain was the thought that I would soon be getting back to my flat in Monte Carlo, to my crisp white sheets and hot water and to all the women who were only too happy to come into my bed. That is how it is, Massimo, he said to me, when you are young you are a butterfly, you flit from flower to flower, and that is as it should be, because unless you do so you will not know what flower it is you eventually want to alight on. The cathedral of Orvieto rises high above the town and of course once you are up there you have a spectacular view of the surrounding countryside. I do not want you to look at the scenery, Massimo, he said to me, I want you to concentrate on the pillars of the west front, where we are standing. There are four of them and on them you will see what is perhaps the greatest sculptural masterpiece of the Italian Middle Ages. Yet we are alone here, he said, while the sheep lie on their backs on their benches gazing up at the monstrosity that is the ceiling of the Sistine Chapel. That is what we have to put up with, Massimo, he said to me, that is the idiocy of our fellow citizens and of our fellow human beings. No matter. We are here. I am no longer young, Massimo, he said, it costs me an effort to get up here, but get up here I have, and this is my reward. The entire history of the world according to the medieval Christian viewpoint, from its creation to the Last Judgement, carved in stone and still almost as perfect as when it was first made, the fronds of the Tree of Jesse as fresh as any tree in spring, the folds of our Lord's cloak as loose and flowing as you will see in any Arab street. What brings us close to tears, Massimo, he said, is the total selflessness of these artists. They were not interested in showing off their noses, he said, and they were not interested in giving interviews and attending festivals. No, he said, they were interested in reaching down into the heart of the mystery and bringing it out into the light of day, undefiled, still mysterious. And because of that, he said, they survive, because of that they fill us with wonder. Wonder, Massimo, he said, without wonder life is nothing. Without wonder we are ants. Everything about us is a cause for wonder, Massimo, he said. A woman. Her elbow. Her wrist. A tree. Its leaves. Its smell. A sound. A memory. And the person who can help us to wonder is the artist. That is why the artist is sacred, he said. *L'artiste est sacré et l'a toujours été.* I can hear him saying it: *L'artiste est sacré, Massimo, et l'a toujours été.* Among the Ife he said, everyone has his allotted task, but the most sacred task is that of the witchdoctor. What you must realise, Daniel said to me, he said, is that these people bathe in the waters of the sacred. When Frobenius came here he could not believe that a

so-called primitive people could carve heads like that. What
Frobenius did not realise, he said, was that *we* are the primitives,
we are the barbarians. Classical Athens was a disaster for the
West, he said. And classical Rome even more so. It turned us
all into barbarians, he said. It removed us from the sacred and
so cut us off from our roots. Plato was a disaster, he said.
Pericles was a disaster. Cicero was a disaster. Caesar was a
disaster. All of them disasters. However hot it was, however
heavy the rains, he said, Daniel always seemed to have a fresh
shirt on, he always looked cool and as though he had come
straight from the barber's. As a Sicilian, he said, I thought I
would be able to cope with the heat, but it is the combination
of heat and damp which is so difficult to cope with in West
Africa. On our first trip I was ill for seventeen of the twenty-
nine days we were there, he said. I had not learned, as Daniel
instinctively knew, how to reset my spiritual clock to these alien
conditions. I learned a lesson, Massimo, he said, a lesson which
has stood me in good stead ever since. It is the spiritual clock
inside you which is important, not the physical conditions
outside you. A man who knows how to set his spiritual clock,
Massimo, he said, is a man who can deal with the world. He is
a man who can make the most of his potential. I must have
known this, Massimo, he said to me that day as we sat in a café
after visiting the cathedral, I must have known this but in the
excitement of youth I had forgotten it. Daniel and the Ife helped
me to remember it. His face was grey, as it often was in those
days, from his exertions, first in climbing up to the cathedral
and then in talking in so impassioned a way about the sculptures on the pillars of the façade. Sometimes when he drank a
glass of water I watched his cheeks sink inwards so that it

seemed as if his face was all bone, but I took care not to let him see me looking, he would not have liked it. Once, it was towards the end, I found him lying on the floor of the living room. I helped him to a chair but he did not seem to know where he was. I asked him if he was all right but he just stared at me. I did not know what to do. I asked him if I should call a doctor, but he just went on staring at me. I was beside myself. I did not want to ring for Annamaria because I felt he would prefer to be seen in this state by as few people as possible. But on the other hand I thought perhaps something irrevocable had happened and he needed to be taken to hospital as quickly as possible. Then, as I was thinking all these contradictory thoughts, he suddenly said, without moving, thank you, Massimo, a glass of water please. I ran to get it for him and by the time I had come back he had straightened his clothes and was sitting in a more natural position. Sit down, Massimo, he said, when he had drunk a little. I asked him where he would like me to sit, I had not sat in his *salotto* before. He motioned me to a chair opposite him. Why is it, Massimo, he said to me, that men are so ashamed of being seen to be vulnerable? It is not as if others do not know it, since we all come down to the same thing in the end. What was my overriding feeling when Arabella left me? It was shame. I was so ashamed I could not be alone by myself and I could not bear to see anyone. In earlier days, he said, when she had left me in London and in Paris, I had gone after her to drag her back, to make her realise the folly of her ways. But this time I knew it was final. And I never saw her or heard from her again, he said, sitting on the upright chair in his *salotto*. After she left me in Switzerland in 1945, just after the war ended, he said, as if she had been waiting for the war to end to make her escape, after she left me, he said, it was as if she had never been, but she left me in a state of profound shame. I thought of that, Massimo, he said, when I opened my eyes just now and saw you looking at me with fear in your eyes. I knew I should never have been in this position, I should never have subjected you to this fear. But it happened. I don't know how it happened, but it happened. One minute I was standing up, I was crossing the room, my mind was busy on important things, and the next I was opening my eyes and seeing you standing there looking at me with undisguised terror. Our mothers help us to stand upright, Massimo, he said, and then they help us to walk. But one day, when our mothers are gone, we find we can no longer stand up. We can no longer walk. One moment we are in full possession of our faculties, we are walking across the carpet of our room, thinking deep thoughts, and the next we are being picked up off the floor by our manservant. What is so shameful about that? he said. It will happen to all of us unless by great good fortune we are run over by a car instead, or kicked in the head by a horse, when we are in the prime of life. The road to the final end is a long one these days, Massimo, he said, with the advances in medicine and the advances in drugs and all the rest of it. It is a road paved with shame, Massimo, he said, especially for someone who is as proud as I am. But it is a road I have to travel and I should get used to it, shouldn't I? You are silent, Massimo, he said. You do not know what to say. And the truth is that there is nothing to say. When we lose control of ourselves, Massimo, he said, we are ashamed even in front of our mothers. How much more ashamed will we be in front of strangers. And yet, Massimo, if someone like me, who prides himself on his realism and on his openness to experience, who, it is no exaggeration to say, spends the greater part of his days and nights opening himself to the experience of the Other, if someone like that cannot accept that what age will bring with it is a loss of control, leading inevitably to a state akin to that of earliest childhood, of babyhood even, if I cannot accept that, who can accept it? Go, Massimo, he said, and say nothing of what has happened to Annamaria or to anyone else. Of course I did what he said and neither of us ever referred to that episode again, but these things have an effect on one, you understand, sir. Our relationship was never quite the same again, if you know what I mean.

He was silent.

— Go on, I said.

— What I mean, sir, is that after that, whenever I was with him, whenever I drove him anywhere or entered his study, not his work study, for no one was allowed to enter that, but his business study, if you understand what I mean, sir, whenever I entered his study to receive his instructions, or saw him come down the stairs to get into the car, I could not help thinking of that day and so in a sense I was seeing two people, if you see what I mean, sir, I was seeing the gentleman I had always known, an aristocrat, a Sicilian aristocrat at that, and I was also seeing the person I had found on the floor and who had opened his eyes and stared at me and did not seem to recognise me. That's the way it is, sir. Like on the television when you are watching a game of football and somehow something has happened to the set and you see two of everything, so you see forty-four players and two referees and two balls, it was a bit like that with Mr Pavone after I had found him on the floor.

He stopped.

I waited for him to resume.

After a while, since he showed no sign of doing so, I said:
Go on.

— It is hard for me to go on, sir.

— Do you want to rest?

— No, sir.

— All right then, go on.

— What would you like me to say, sir?

— Was he aware of a change in your relationship?

— I cannot tell, sir.

— Go on.

— I tried to act as I had always acted, sir. When we stopped
for a picnic on one of our drives out into the countryside I made
sure I did not fuss around him more than I had previously done.
I did not want to embarrass him.

— Of course. Go on.

— What do you want me to say, sir?

— Why did Miss Mauss say she would not go on working
in the same house as you? I asked him.

— I cannot say, sir.

— Had you and Miss Mauss quarrelled?

— We had nothing to do with each other.

— Do you know why she left Mr Pavone's employment?

— No, sir.

— Mr Pavone said nothing to you about it?

— No, sir.

— And Annamaria?

— I don't understand, sir.

— She said nothing about it either?

— I told you, sir, people came and went in Mr Pavone's
employment. It was none of our business.

— How did you get on personally with Miss Mauss?

— We had nothing to do with each other.

— All right. Go on.

— About what, sir?

— What else did Mr Pavone say about Monte Carlo and his time there?

— He said that by 1927, when he was twenty-two, he had had enough of it. He had met Daniel Bernstein by then, he said. With Daniel, he said, I went walking in the Swiss Alps. I had my fill of mountains in those years, he said. I do not have a German or an Austrian soul and for me the mountains are a source of pleasure pure and simple, not a gateway to the world of the spirit. Bach did not go to the mountains, he said. Mozart did not go to the mountains. Listen to their music. It dances. It sings. And then listen to the music of a dedicated mountain-goer like Mahler and you see what a disaster for music mountains have been. That music neither sings nor dances, it crawls on its belly and imagines it is rising to the stars. The mountains of Nepal and Tibet, he said, are something else. Nobody in the mountains of Nepal or Tibet has the slightest interest in mountains. In fact they are terrified of mountains. On every high pass, he said, you will see a cairn with messages on it to keep away the evil spirits of the mountains. Ascetics will sit down and chant, tapping on their drums, when they are about to cross a high pass, he said, so as to keep the evil powers at bay. In 1927, he said, I went with Daniel to West Africa, to the kingdom of the Ife. His great friend, Oba Adesoji Aderemi, was the Ooni or headman of Ife at that time. Frobenius had been there a few years earlier and excavated a number of sites, but the Ooni was keen to show us not only the past but the present of his kingdom. He showed us the Ore Grove on the outskirts of the city, an ancient sacred site still used then as a place of worship. There is a mysterious figure standing there, he said, his features rubbed away by time, his hands clasped round his stomach, protecting a sort of pouch which hangs there. Some say he is a dwarf who represents the hunter deity, others that he is Ore's servant. Ore, he said, was said to beckon visitors from a distance with laughter and spontaneous joy. If any visitor responded in the same way, however, his facial features, it was said, would remain permanently fixed in a contorted grimace. That, he said, is the negation of the human, it is the embodiment of evil. Think, Massimo, of the newborn baby, he said. He learns to smile by seeing his mother smile, he learns to laugh by seeing his mother laugh. He learns that he has laughter inside him because he sees it in the face of a loved and trusted being who is always with him. This figure is a denial of all that. What is it trying to tell, Massimo? he said. What is it trying to tell us? Next to it, as you enter the grove, are two stone slabs, vaguely fish-like in form. One is said to be a mudfish. These fish, he said, using their secondary lung system, bury themselves in mud during the dry season and appear to be reborn when the rains come and the waters rise. For that reason, Massimo, he said to me, the mudfish is a sacrificial offering among the Yoruba of Ife, greatly prized for its name, *aja ajabo*, which means 'a fish that fights for its life'. The other slab is said to represent the crocodile. Crocodiles are regarded by the Yoruba as warriors of the water and are said to be messengers of the gods of the lagoons. The crocodile, the Ooni explained to us, represents the time when the world was all water. The greatest stone carving of Ore, he said, is one I have already talked to you about before, Massimo, because it made such an impression on me. It is the granite obelisk, standing almost two and a half meters high, with five holes bored into it running from near the middle to the top. In that block of granite we find a miracle taking place, he said. For what we have here is pure stone, primal matter, which has been touched, but only touched, by the human. In the normal course of things, Massimo, he said, for the human to leave a trace upon the earth is to civilise it, and thus to weaken it. But the marks of the human, in this case, he said, the cutting of this massive block of granite and the boring into it of five holes, is so minimal, and has been carried out with so much respect for the materiality of the stone, that it takes nothing away from its primal power. Quite the reverse. It is almost as though the making of these marks, which do not show the sign of the human hand of course, which might almost be created by nature herself, almost but not quite, have, paradoxically, only reinforced the inhuman, telluric quality of the granite. Our civilisation could not have done this, Massimo, he said. Only a civilisation which instinctively understood the authority of the telluric could have produced something as awesome as this.

— What did he mean by the telluric? I asked him.

— I do not know, sir, he said. That was what Mr Pavone said.

— All right, I said. Go on.

— That block of granite, Massimo, he said to me, was like a call to arms. For the first time since as a child I had attacked the piano with all my energy and with my whole body, I felt the stirrings of something deep within me. I did not know what to do with these stirrings, he said. I did not know how to respond to them. But the sense of that so-called Shield of Ore and the excitement, the confusion, it caused inside me, I never forgot. *Je n'ai jamais oublié le bouleversement que la vue de cet objet a produit en moi, Massimo. Jamais.* It was to be another twenty-five years before I knew what to do with that feeling, he said, but it was there, and it made me abandon first Monte Carlo and its waltzes, then London and its glittering society, and drove me eventually to Scheler in Vienna. But that was a false start, he said to me. We were inspecting his shoes. This happened once a year, when he gave away to charity those shoes he no longer wished to wear. I picked them up and put them in a large box as he pointed his stick. That was a false start, Massimo, he said. A dead end. I had to go back to the beginning and start all over again, and I would never have got started in the right direction had it not been for my trip with Tucci to Nepal in 1949, he said. When I went to Nepal, he said, I had long forgotten the Shield of Ore, he said, but in Nepal I remembered it again. It has been the lodestar of my life, he said. It is not too much to say that it has been the lodestar of my life. Some of the shoes he had not worn even once, others he had worn so much that there was no life left in them whatever. I could tell the pain it caused him when he would point to one such pair and say: That one, Massimo, and I would take them up and put them in the box. But he showed no emotion. Mr Pavone was not someone who showed emotion. That one, Massimo, he said. And that one. And that one. It was the same with the shirts and the ties and even the suits, but he was less attached to those than to his shoes. A good bed, Massimo, he would say, and a good pair of shoes, that is all a man needs. Not that he was not concerned with his shirts and his ties and his suits. We must present ourselves to the god of music, he would say, as to any other god, dressed in the best possible way. Any sloppiness in dress, Massimo, he would say, will be reflected in sloppiness of composition. I will not tolerate sloppiness, Massimo, he would say, in you or in anyone who works for me, just as I will not tolerate sloppiness in anyone who plays my music. My wife, Massimo, he would say, was one of the most beautiful women in the world and she was always immaculately dressed. But in her soul she was a slut. It took me a long time to accept that, he said, but it's the truth, and the day comes when we have to face the truth, no matter how uncomfortable. She bathed in milk when that was the fashion, he said, gallons and gallons of milk, she filled her bath to over-flowing, she wallowed in it and let it soak into her skin. And she did indeed have the most silken skin, Massimo, he said. I would have given a great deal to touch that skin, to stroke that skin, as would any man, he said. And indeed I did give a great deal. I gave my life. A mistake, Massimo, he said, but I have no regrets. To regret, Massimo, he said, is to admit that one should have acted differently. But at the time the choice did not present itself. The wedding took place in Buckingham Palace, he said, for she was a niece of the Queen of England. There is no more depressing building, Massimo, he said to me, than Buckingham Palace. It is grey outside and it is grey inside. It is filled with the most atrocious furniture. Even the paintings on the walls, which include some of the world's greatest masterpieces, are badly hung and difficult to see. But that doesn't matter because nobody who lives or works in Buckingham Palace wants to see them. They have always been there, as far as they are concerned, and they will always be there. If one of them were to go missing there would be an almighty fuss, but only because walls need to have paintings, and the bigger the wall the bigger the painting.

Kings have always had the most atrocious taste, Massimo, he said, the only people with worst taste than kings are tyrants and dictators. I did not want to be married in Buckingham Palace, he said, I did not want to eat those cucumber sandwiches for which Buckingham Palace is famous, but it was what my wife wanted and when we are in love, Massimo, we do the most absurd things to please the loved one. He pointed with his stick and I put another pair of shoes in the box. The first time she left me, Massimo, he said, I found her in Oxford, staying with an uncle of hers, a clergyman, who was attached to one of the colleges there. He was a papyrologist. He offered me a glass of sherry, but I declined. Pack your bags, I said to her, the car is waiting outside. The papyrologist suggested we sit down and talk, but there was nothing to talk about. In the car on the way back to London she cried and begged me to forgive her. She had a way of crying silently, her body shaking and tears streaming down her face but not a sound coming out of her. It wrung my heart, Massimo, he said, to witness her when the crying fit was really upon her. But as soon as we returned to London the old quarrels broke out again. She accused me of not loving her in the manner in which she obscurely felt she deserved to be loved. I paid no attention to all this and for a while we carried on as before. I was writing poetry in Italian and playing Couperin on the harpsichord. I had discovered the poems of Belli, that nineteenth-century Roman poet who wrote the most witty and scabrous poems in the Roman dialect. I toyed with the idea of writing a comic opera on the *Phèdre* of Racine, set in Rome in the nineteenth century and with the characters speaking *romagnolo* and the music consisting of popular tunes of the 1920s. I played polo with the English aristocracy and with the jumped-up sons of brewers. To tell you the truth, Massimo, he said, as he motioned with his stick and I picked up another pair of shoes and added them to the pile in the box, I was bored. Unhappy and bored. I arranged to have my opera put on, but the English musical establishment, the most conservative musical establishment in the world, turned up their noses at it. All apart from the Sitwells and Lord Berners. It was then I decided to go to Vienna and seek out Schoenberg or one of his pupils. I was tired of frivolity, Massimo, he said. I was twenty-six years old and I needed to go down into the heart of music, to find something that was more than glitter and cynical humour. Over my dead body, my wife said. She was a dreadful linguist, like all the English, and the thought of living in Vienna terrified her. Besides, she had a stream of lovers or perhaps they were only admirers. I do not think she was interested enough in sex to have a stream of lovers, so it was probably a stream of admirers, whom she would have been loath to leave. So I went on my own. I found a flat next door to the opera house and I set about finding the best teacher I could. Arabella wrote me a letter a week, sheet after sheet in her childish hand, telling me about all the balls and race meetings she had been to and sailing at cows and cricket with the lords and shooting in the Highlands on weekends in this grand house and that, with this lover or admirer or that. Thursday mornings, that was the day these letters arrived, these extraordinary missives, which seemed to have been written by someone who had never heard of censorship or revision, she wrote in exactly the same way of her premenstrual pains, she had always been given to premenstrual pains, as of her dinner parties, of her constipation as of the golden down on the arm of the latest young man to fall in love with her. It would take me a week to read through these letters. I had only just got to the end of one when the next one arrived. What I felt was that she was living for both of us and so I could take a break from living and concentrate on music. But Scheler was a big disappointment. At first I thought it was my fault, he said, then I thought that perhaps I had chosen the wrong teacher, but the more I talked to the musicians of Vienna the more I realised they were all infected with this intellectual disease. They were all obsessed with reason and analysis, with words like Necessity and Truth. The best of them, like Schoenberg and Berg, used this as a way of harnessing their hysterical emotion. Because they were all hysterics. Jewish hysterics. Even when they were not Jews, like Webern, who was the best of them, they were infected with the Jewish hysteria. At the same time the papers were like buckets full of excrement, Massimo, he said, you have no idea of the way Jews were vilified in a so-called centre of world civilisation like Vienna, it was not surprising they felt they needed to retreat into Reason and Science. Only that which was reasonable and that which was scientific would release them from the smells that came up from the sewers of Vienna. It was not a place to be, Massimo, he said, if you were Italian, if you were Sicilian. Arabella had been right not to wish to come with me, Massimo, he said. When Hitler came to power in Germany in 1933 it got even worse. I did not want to have anything to do with people like Scheler and even with Schoenberg, he said, I did not want to have anything to do with Viennese intellectuals and artists, all suicides, actual and potential, and I did not want to have anything to do with Hitler and his Viennese disciples or with Mussolini and his thugs. So I returned to London. But London no longer satisfied me, he said. The Court of St James no longer satisfied me. Oysters at Wheeler's and weekends in the country no longer satisfied me. I decided to settle in Paris, still a civilised city in the midst of all this excrement. But before we could move Arabella disappeared again. I made enquiries and found that she had taken herself off to New York. In these situations, Massimo, he said, it is essential to act decisively. I took the next boat for New York. I had a loaded pistol in my pocket. I am not sure whether I intended to shoot her or to shoot myself in front of her. In the event I tracked her down to a hotel in Greenwich Village and sat there in the bar drinking and waiting for her to come in. After a long time a man came up to me and asked if I was the Italian lord. I said yes. A lady would like to see you, he said. What kind of a lady? I asked. A lady, he said, and gave me the key to a room. I went upstairs. I had the gun in the pocket of my jacket and I kept one hand on it. With the other I inserted the key the man had given me into the lock. It was very quiet in the hotel, four o'clock in the afternoon. The door to the bedroom was open and I walked across the thick carpet and stood in the doorway. The curtains were drawn, but there was just enough light to see by. She was lying on the bed with her face to the wall. I stood for a long time by the door, looking. Finally I walked across and sat down on the bed beside her. Neither of us said a word. A long time passed. It grew dark but we stayed on like that. Then she turned over and opened her eyes and looked at me. She had eyes like no one else, Massimo, he said. Violet eyes. Like no one else. The return journey across the Atlantic was our veritable honeymoon, Massimo, he said. We were closer then than at any other time. Closer than we would ever be again. So we moved to Paris and

I met Jouve and Eluard and Michaux and all the rest of them and began to write poetry in French. But I was lost, Massimo, he said, lost. I didn't want to spend my life writing waltzes of the kind I had written in Monte Carlo, amusing as those had been to write, and I didn't want to write the sorts of serial compositions Scheler had been trying to get me to write. But beyond that I knew nothing. And then things got very bad in Europe. It was impossible to stay in Paris and there was no question of moving back to Rome, so we went to Switzerland, three days before the war broke out. At least in Switzerland you could leave the shouting behind and try to lead a civilised life. But you cannot lead a civilised life when you know what is happening all around you. You can take walks in the mountains and breathe in the good air, but you cannot shut out reality. Had I been able to write music I might have done so, he said. But I could no longer write. I sat at my piano and I played the same note, over and over again, hour after hour, the same note. Arabella begged me to stop but I could not leave the piano alone and I could not play anything except that one note. So in order to spare her I signed myself in to a sanatorium. My health was very bad anyway, and I thought, Europe is a madhouse, so the only way to stay sane is to enter a madhouse. Because these Swiss sanatoria are all madhouses, Massimo, he said. Believe me, he said, I tried dozens of them. All madhouses. The doctors are mad and the nurses are mad and the patients are mad. In one of them I led a revolt of the patients against the management. We were being treated like vermin even though we were paying through the nose, and I decided a stand must be taken. We took the senior doctor hostage, a madman called Schweinsteiger, and we locked him in a dark room until the management acceded to our requests. In another I organised a music festival, he said. I formed a choir and I taught them how to make various animal sounds and we put all those together and a rather interesting piece of music emerged. We all enjoyed ourselves thoroughly and the patients who took part immediately got better, but when we performed it in public for the other patients and the doctors and nurses they booed us so loudly we had to stop. However, all the performers discharged themselves the next day, their symptoms had entirely disappeared. I stayed on because I preferred to be inside than outside, but everyone blamed me for the concert and the management blamed me for persuading the performers that they were cured. It was then I realised, Massimo, he said, that there is no such thing as informed listening to music, there is only prejudice and the absence of prejudice. Why are the sounds of twenty-eight animals all barking and braying and mooing and hooting in concert any less beautiful than Bach's B Minor Mass or the last movement of the Ninth Symphony? Tell me that, Massimo, he said, tell me that and I will give you a doctorate in music.

He was silent.

– Go on, I said.

– Yes, sir, he said.

I waited.

Finally I said: What else did he say about the Swiss sanatoria?

– Switzerland, he said to me once, is not as dull as people make it out to be. There is more to Switzerland than cheese and sanatoria and mountains, he said. There are more drunks and there are more suicides in Swizerland than in any other European country. And there are more madmen per head of the population than in any other European country. I met some remarkable individuals, he said, both inside the sanatoria and outside. I met some remarkable mad billiard-players, with whom I played billiards for hours at a time in the sanatoria. We had no cues, we had to use our hands, our arms and our hands. We played for hours at a time. Sometimes we had no balls either, because of the war there were shortages even in Switzerland. Shortage of billiard cues and even of billiard balls. What went on in these sanatoria, I can't tell you, he said. The patients with each other. The doctors and nurses with each other. The doctors and nurses with the patients. Such goings-on. In these sanatoria one could do anything. So long as one did not talk about the war. Everybody had to pretend there was no war. It was enough to drive you mad. Whenever I could I played the piano. Just one note. Always one note. He's madder than the rest, they said. But it's by playing one note over and over again that you get to the heart of that note. I didn't realise it then, I accepted what they said, that I was madder than the rest, although a part of me was always aware that I was not mad at all. In the end, he said, I could not stand those sanatoria any more and I got out. I rejoined Arabella in our flat in Geneva and I spent the day looking out of the window at the lake and waiting for the war to end. Arabella too was waiting for it to end. As soon as it ended she disappeared again. A friend offered to try and find out where she had gone, but I no longer wanted to know. From that day to this, Massimo, he said, I have not heard from her, nor have I made any attempt to find her. It is as if she had never existed, he said. Never existed. For a while I wondered if there would be any news of her but there was none. She had been swallowed up into thin air, he said. Into thin air.

He was silent for a long time. I let him be. Then I said: Go on.

— How? he said.

— What happened after she left?

— I knew I could not stay in Geneva any more, he said, sitting in my flat by the lake and playing that one note over and over again. I felt that I had reached a turning point in my life, but I did not know what it was. We were driving to San Felice, he liked to have lunch in the Circeo Park Hotel, looking out over the sea. So I left Geneva and settled in Paris again, he said, I already knew many of the writers and artists there. The Surrealists. Ponge. Giacometti. Sartre. Above all Michaux. Michaux was a lovely man. When his wife died he began to draw and paint. I wanted to escape from words, he said. I wanted to escape from the control of words. I wanted my hand to lead me, my pencil to lead me. Later he took mescalin and painted what he saw when he was high on mescalin, but in those days he was still mourning his wife. In Paris a funny thing happened to me, Mr Pavone said. I held my hand up to my face and I could not recognise it. Not only did I not see that it was a hand, I did not know that it belonged to me. I wanted to cry all the time but not a tear would drop. *Pas une larme*, Massimo, he said. *Pas une larme*. I was at work on a huge orchestral piece, still in the serial style I thought was necessary for any serious composition. It was called *The Eternal Silence of Those Infinite Spaces*. My body was screaming at me to stop but my will forced me to go on. My shoulder was paralysed. I had to get someone to help with the copying of the score. Every day when I woke up all I wanted was to stay in bed, to cover my face with the blankets and shut out the day. But I forced myself to get up. I forced myself to sit at my desk. I forced myself to complete *The Eternal Silence of Those Infinite Spaces*. And finally it was done. Monteux was to conduct it. I wanted to run away but conventions are conventions, Massimo, he said, and so I forced myself into my black tie and I took a taxi to the Salle Pleyel. But I could not go into the hall. I rushed to the lavatory and was sick. Afterwards I lay on the floor to try and recover. Strains of music came to my ears. My music. It made me feel sick. Then suddenly the door was flung open and someone was looking at me. He began to shout: *There's a dead man here! There's a dead man here!* I got up at once and motioned to him to be quiet. Then I heard the last chords and the sound of clapping, so I pushed him aside and ran to the auditorium and slipped in, walked slowly forward as if from the back and climbed onto the podium and embraced Monteux and the leader and clapped the orchestra and took my bow. After that I asked them to get me a taxi and went straight back to my room and did not move from my bed for three weeks. Jouve suggested I become one of his wife's patients but I would sooner have been treated by a baboon than by that woman. He thought he could add to the slave population, Massimo, he said to me that day as we drove to the Circeo Park Hotel where he had reserved a table for us on the terrace, over-looking the sea. He thought that by helping me to get my poems published in French he had found his wife another slave. That was when I made up my mind to go to Nepal, he said. I went to Nepal to flee the threat of slavery to Mme Pierre Jean Jouve, but it turned out that Nepal was my destiny, as deafness had been the destiny of Beethoven. Nepal was my destiny and my salvation, Massimo, he said. When Tucci invited me to join his expedition I did not hesitate for a moment, he said. Everything about those four months was extraordinary, he said. It was as if I had been put into one of those washing machines, not a day went by when I was not pummelled and whirled around by forces greater than myself. I did not know what was happening to me, Massimo, he said, as we sat on the terrace overlooking the sea and had one of those meals for which the Circeo Park Hotel is famous. I did not know what was happening but I clung on, he said. Perhaps a caterpillar feels like this as it begins to turn into a butterfly, he said. As I stood in the courtyards of the temples and heard the enormous trumpets blaring out I felt the walls of my being crumble and I did not know if I would come out of it alive or if I would give up the ghost there in Nepal and disappear for ever. I knew only that I had to cling on, Massimo, he said. The Circeo Park Hotel is renowned for its fish and Mr Pavone was a great eater of fish. The walls of my inner being, Massimo, he said, as he dissected his fish, and also the walls of my outer being. I felt like a molten lump of metal being beaten into shape by some mighty force, he said. The heat was intense, Massimo, he said. The beating was beyond my endurance. Something new was being forged, Massimo he said. Far beyond endurance. But I knew it was my destiny, he said, so I rejoiced at the same time as I despaired of ever getting out of there alive. Here I was, on the cusp of the lowlands and the highlands, for Nepal is the bridge between the two, between the arable fields to the south and the arid mountains to the north, here I was, being heated till I began to melt and then being beaten into a new shape, he said. The hills were full of blossom, he said, and the monkeys darted from tree to tree, and everywhere you went you heard the sound of chanting. Of chanting, Massimo, he said, not singing. Do you know the difference between singing and chanting, Massimo? he said. Because if you do not you cannot hope to understand my music. To sing is to begin at the beginning and to go on to the end and then to stop. To chant is to align yourself with the rhythms of the universe. Singing goes somewhere, he said, chant is already there. Singing is for young ladies, Massimo, he said, and for the preening divas of the opera house. Chanting is for monks. When you begin to chant, Massimo, he said, you are taken over by a force greater than any you have ever known. It runs through you from the tip of your toe to the top of your head. Your whole body tingles, Massimo, he said, your chest heaves, you are no longer yourself, you are part of the chanting. One can become addicted to chanting, Massimo, he said, as one can become addicted to drink or to drugs. After a certain time the body cannot do without it. The only difference is that chanting cannot kill you as drink and drugs can. After lunch we took a little walk along the sea, in the great gardens of the hotel. He had fallen silent. And in the car on the way back to Rome he did not utter a word. I do not know whether this was out of tiredness or because he was thinking. He would often be silent for the whole of our drives, I knew he was thinking about his music. He found, he told me, as he grew older, that going out for a drive was a good way to resolve a musical problem. No problem without a solution, Massimo, he said. But the problem may of course have been wrongly posed in the first place. That was the trouble with Schoenberg and Scheler and his other disciples. They thought they had found the solution, but it was the solution to the wrong problem. When I came back from Nepal, he said, I sat down at the piano in my house here and I played the same note, over and over again, hour after hour and

day after day, just as I had done in Switzerland. But the difference was this, Massimo, he said to me. I no longer felt this to
be an admission of defeat. On the contrary, he said, I understood it was a sign of triumph. I played that one note and as I
played I listened. I listened and I understood. At that moment
a new kind of music was born. The first piece I called *Six Sixty-
Six. Six Sixty-Six.* The same note struck in the same way on the
piano six hundred and sixty-six times. It was beautiful,
Massimo, he said. Its beauty was an otherworldly beauty. It
would either drive you mad or draw you into another dimen-
sion. When it was performed later, by Pollini at Dartington,
and then at Bregenz, the audience rioted, and walked out. Cage
said to me: This is a piece I would like to have written if only
I had thought of it. But he was wrong. He could never have
written it. I was fond of Cage, he said, he had an inkling of the
way of the Buddha, but fatally contaminated by American New
Ageism. He never understood my music. If he had written *Six
Sixty-Six* he would have been content with the idea, he would
have been indifferent to the sound. Whereas I was not interested in the idea, he said, I was interested in the sound.
Suddenly, he said, what had been a barrier between me and what
I wanted to say became precisely the thing that I wanted to say.
What Nepal taught me, he said, was that what we are striving
for is not *transcendence* but *transformation.* The world is there to be
transformed. The human being is there to be *transformed.* Not tran-
scended, *transformed.* When a note is played six hundred and
sixty-six times it is *transformed.* The ear that hears the same note
six hundred and sixty-six times is *transformed.* All my life, he said,
I had felt this urge to eat the world because I loved it so much,
to eat it and ingest it and make it a part of me. It was the same

with women, Massimo, he said to me. Eat and ingest, eat and
ingest. But of course you cannot eat the world, Massimo, he
said. You cannot eat a woman. And so you fall back, frustrated
and despondent, until the urge seizes you again, and again you
make the effort and again you fail. But when I came back from
Nepal, after I had been hurled about and shaken in the great
washing machine of Nepal, he said, I found that all the problems, all the barriers, had fallen away. Instead of striking the
same note again and again in frustration, I wrote *Six Sixty-Six*.
The performer of the piece has to take his time. The pacing
must be absolutely even. It is intolerable to listen to, he said. It
is intolerable to play. Why? Because it is so close to ecstasy. The
second piece I wrote, he said, another piano piece, *Heraclitus*,
could not have been mistaken for Cage. The first section had
the superscription: 'What was scattered, gathers; what was gathered, scatters.' The second: 'Under the comb, the tangle and the
straight path are the same.' The third: 'The sun is new, all day.'
Each section lasts less than a minute, he said. But when Pollini
played them in Bregenz they had a greater effect on the audience than Mahler's *Song of the Earth*. One person had a fit. Another
began to take off all her clothes. When I wrote those pieces, he
said, I was glacially calm, but I knew I had arrived at last. Instead
of being my enemy, with whom I had to fight every inch of the
way, as it had seemed when I worked with Scheler in Vienna,
he said, music had become my friend, with whom I was happy
to spend long hours. A sound is not a step on the way to something else, he said, but it is itself a universe in which we should
be happy to set up our dwelling. I, who had never felt at home
anywhere, he said, was now made to feel at home by music. In
those early years of my return from Nepal, he said, of my reset-

tling in Rome after all those years away, I was drunk with possibility. I could not spend enough hours at my desk, my piano. I would work from early morning far into the night and sometimes I would not go to bed till dawn, and a few hours later I would be back at my desk, at my piano. It was as if the barriers had been broken and the waters were rushing out, sweeping me before them, and it was as much as I could do to keep my head above the water. Some days I did not eat at all, he said, and some nights I did not sleep at all, but I always made sure I was well-dressed and that my clothes were clean and well-pressed. Always. Nor was I in a hurry, he said. When you have entered the world of music, he said, when you are penetrating to the heart of each sound, then time ceases to matter. You are no longer working with time and you are no longer working in time. Each sound in itself, he said. Each passing moment in itself. That is the secret, Massimo, he said. That is the secret. The composer is not a craftsman, Massimo, he said to me. He is not a genius. He is a conduit, a go-between. A postman. That is what he has been chosen for. It is no reflection on his character that he is chosen, it is simply a fact. I was chosen, Massimo, he said to me, and I had to do what I was chosen for, just as you were chosen to help me in my task. Fortunately everything conspired to make that possible, he said. Everything from my upbringing in the great house in Sicily to my years in Monte Carlo, to my meeting with my wife and our many stormy years together in London and Paris and Switzerland, to her leaving me and my despair and my trip with Tucci to Nepal. After his stroke he talked more and more about the shape of his life. We cannot foretell how any of it will turn out, Massimo, he said, but when we look back everything seems fated. Everything

seems to have had a purpose. Even the absurdity of being born
into a Sicilian noble family, the most ridiculous fate anyone
could wish for. Artists have always come from the middle
classes, he said. Very few have been aristocrats. Being born into
the aristocracy is a terrible handicap, he said. Look at Lord
Berners. He was a gifted man who was ruined by his class and
his caste. The middle classes are both more ambitious and more
hard-working, Massimo, he said, that is why the bulk of artists,
from Dante to Shakespeare and from Beethoven to Thomas
Mann, have come from that class. The only trouble with the
middle class is its tendency to avoid risk. I, on the other hand,
have always taken risks. You could say that I love risk. From
the beginning I was frightened of nothing, he said. That has
always stood me in good stead. I was not afraid to write waltzes
for the palm court orchestras of Monte Carlo, and I was not
afraid to tell Scheler that I did not feel he had anything to teach
me. From the beginning I felt you were wasting my time, Scheler
retorted. From the beginning I felt that your damned Italian
and Sicilian aristocratic arrogance would never allow you to
make the most of your undoubted talents. Your undoubted
talents, he said, for he prided himself on his fair-mindedness.
It was no use telling him he was barking up the wrong tree, that
he was leading his pupils into a dead end, he would not have
understood me. We parted if not amicably at least with enormous politeness on both sides, a Sicilian aristocratic politeness
on my side and a Viennese Jewish politeness on his. Poor
Scheler, he said, he was not fortunate enough to escape to
America like his master. His wife was ailing and he stayed,
though his friends had found him a post at Buffalo. I heard later
that he had been deported and killed, he and his wife and all

his family. A cesspit, Massimo, he said. Europe was a cesspit in those years. And the stink has not entirely disappeared. In Italy, at any rate, they still long for a strong man to lead them, a man with an iron chin. We have not seen the end of it, Massimo, he said. When I go to Hungary and Romania to hear my music played I hear about the monstrousness of the gypsies. When I go to Belgrade I hear about the smell left by the Turks and the Bosnians. When I go to Poland I hear about the treachery of the Jews. There's no end to it, Massimo, he said. No end to it. The best place to be is in your study, he said, making music. I have been fortunate, Massimo, he said to me, that all I have ever really been interested in is women and music. For while women can hurt you, they also enrich your life. Even my wife enriched my life. I always recognised that, whatever she did to me, and she did terrible damage to me, he said, she nevertheless, on balance, enriched my life. That is why I have no regrets, Massimo, he said to me. He was lying in his bed, very small and very white. He still dyed his hair so that it was as black as it had always been, but his face was very white. He was still writing his music. I had to prop him up. Annamaria could not do it, she was too old and weak herself. I should get rid of her, he said. If I had any common sense I would get rid of her, but she has been with me for so long I do not have the heart. So I propped him up with all these pillows and placed the plank on his knees and he wrote. When he tired of writing he rang the bell and asked me to sit with him. That is when he talked. I have no regrets, he often said that. It would be foolish to have regrets. Besides, what sort of life was it that I gave her? When we married I still went out into the world, he said. I still played the host when she required me to, and presided over the dinner

parties that she organised. The trouble was that she had a bourgeois soul, despite her filthy aristocratic ways. At heart she was
a bourgeois and I was not, he said. I was an artist. I was only
happy when I was writing music or thinking about music.
Artists should either be married to adoring women who will
put up with anything, like Bach, he said, or they should be
married to remarkable women, like Mozart, or they should not
be married at all. That was what my wife was trying to say to
me when she ran away, he said. At first I did not understand
and I went after her and brought her back, first from Oxford
and then from New York. But when she finally left me at the
end of the war I sensed that was the end. The end of our relationship and the end of my married life. Human beings are such
slow learners, Massimo, he said to me. It takes them years and
years to learn the simplest things. After that, he said, I knew I
was by myself. It is a different thing being by yourself at twenty
and being by yourself at forty, he said. At twenty you are by
yourself because you have not yet found the right person. But
at forty you are by yourself because you have understood that
partnering is not for you. That is a terrible discovery to make,
he said, but it is also a liberating one. The best thing Arabella
did for me was to leave me, he said. In Paris after the war I ran
after every woman I came across except for Mme Pierre Jean
Jouve, but I could sense that the writing was on the wall. Some
of them were so beautiful I was able to forget my destiny for a
while in their embrace. Some of them were so intelligent or so
kind that I was able to bask for a while in their company and
convince myself that they were the partners for me. But I knew
that sooner or later I would have to go away. I would have to
be shaken up or I would simply wither and die. I had no inten-

tion of withering in Paris and dying, he said. There was still too much to do. So I left Paris, I left my dear Henri Michaux, and I went to Nepal with Tucci and Maraini, both remarkable men. Maraini was the photographer, a scholar of Japanese culture as well as of Indian and Tibetan. He had one finger missing from his left hand because during the war in a Japanese prisoner of war camp he had cut it off and cooked it to feed his little daughter. Bartok was another who had a loving wife, he said, but she was not with him in Egypt when I became acquainted with him and with Hindemith at the Congress for World Music which was held there. I had long been interested in that country and Daniel and I spent many happy weeks there before the Congress. At the Congress itself our host was a pupil of Bartok's, who was living in that country. There is a photo he took of me with Bartok and Mr and Mrs Hindemith and with the great Austrian ethnomusicologist Erich von Hornbostel, with the pyramids in the background. Bartok was the sweetest and gentlest of men, he said, but Hindemith was a typical German, with a typical German wife. It was fashionable in those days to go out into the desert with a group of friends and play at being archaeologists. We would find a mound and start to dig and soon we would find all sorts of ancient Egyptian treasures, brooches in the form of scarabs and little statues of the winged sky-god Nut and other deities of ancient Egypt. When you cleaned the dirt off these you would often find, inscribed in a corner, 'Made in Germany'. I have never been in the least interested in the monumental aspect of ancient Egypt, he said. It stinks of Empire and reminds me of the monstrosities built by dictators everywhere, by Mussolini in Rome and Hitler in Berlin and Stalin in Moscow and Ceauşescu in Bucharest. But some of the birds and farmyard animals depicted in the tombs are remarkable, as is the Coptic and Islamic art of Egypt. The folk traditions, both artistic and musical, of that country are remarkable too, he said. But it was to be many years before I understood what it was about it I found moving and how to relate it to my own music. For I am not interested in incorporating folk rhythms into my music, as Bartok was, or the rhythm of Buddhist or Gregorian chanting, as some composers are today. I am interested in finding through my own work what it is that this work has in common with these traditions. Only in that way can we move forward, he said. Anything else is pastiche and no better than the populist and pretentious work of Prokofiev and Shostakovitch, much beloved of those with a sentimental disposition and tin ears. Sometimes I sat with him for the whole day and he said nothing. He lay there with his eyes closed, but if I tried to creep away he would say: No, Massimo, stay. Sometimes without opening his eyes he would say that he no longer needed me that day. I tried to keep his shoes free from dust and to make sure that his suits and shirts were aired, but he no longer went out and often did not even dress, spending the day in bed in his pyjamas, it was difficult to summon the energy and dispiriting, yes, sir, it was a dispiriting thing to do. Those shoes which had been worn so often, those suits, sometimes I had to sit down in the giant cupboard and cry. Some days though he dressed as carefully as ever and sat at his desk, not for long, but he sat at his desk and at the piano. For almost forty years, Massimo, he said to me, I have tried to reach into the heart of sound, and in that time I have written some very great works, but I still feel that the ultimate mystery is eluding me. It is this which compels me to go on composing, he said. That sensation I first experienced in the mountains and valleys of Nepal, he said, of being thrown into a giant washing machine and tumbling and tossing in waters too violent to resist, not knowing if I was on my head or on my feet, it is that which I still experience every time I sit down to compose. That is what is exciting, Massimo, he said, that is what keeps me going, the sense that I must bring it back intact from Over There, give it a form without distracting from its Otherness, from the chaos and violence at its heart. Chaos and order, he said, chaos and order, that has always been what we artists have had to struggle with. Musicians more than most. My *Goat Songs*, which I wrote for Yoko Mitani, is the first proper use of the human voice in Western music for a century and a half, he said. There is nothing more ridiculous, Massimo, he said, than trying to set a text to music. Nobody understands the words and the composer is constrained to move from A to B and then from B to C and so on and so forth. That was well and good when the world itself was conceived as moving from Creation to Last Judgement, but it is not well and good if what you want is to enter right into the heart of the world of sound, not pass lightly over it. To set a text that has a meaning, Massimo, he said, is like walking down the road to reach the police station where you will turn yourself in. Nobody wants to walk down the road, he said. They want to dance in the park. They want to lie in the grass. But they have been brainwashed into believing that they want to walk down that road, and why? Because in the police station at the end of the road sits a man in uniform who will put handcuffs on your wrists and tell you what you have done wrong. My *Goat Songs* by contrast, he said, are designed to return the voice to the body. They do not walk to the police station in order to turn themselves in, and they do not make a virtue out of hissing and spitting and gurgling as these so-called avant-garde composers have learned to do, they have no sense of the sacredness of the body and as a consequence they cannot treat the production of sound inside the body with the reverence it deserves. We cannot write Gregorian chant, he said and we cannot write Buddhist chant, but we can learn from these chants what it is that needs doing with the voice, he said. I spoke to Yoko, he said, before she began to work on the songs. You have been out with friends, I said to her. You have eaten well. You have eaten too well. You begin to feel a bit funny. You begin to feel your stomach acting in an abnormal way. You listen to it. You are no longer aware of the conversation around you. And suddenly you know you have to run to the toilet. You run, you push open the door, you close it behind you, you bend over the bowl and suddenly it all comes out of you, all that you have eaten and more and more and more, everything is coming out of your mouth, and you don't care what sounds you are making so long as you can empty your stomach. I said to her, that is the sound I want from you in the second song. And then I said to her: You have been out for the evening with friends. You climb the stairs to your flat. You insert the key in the lock. You open the door and you go in. You turn and you lock the door. And then, as you are going to put on the light, you become aware of someone, there, in the flat, in the dark, waiting for you. You turn. You see him. You begin to scream. That is what I want from you in the fourth song, I said to her. A scream of sheer terror, of sheer panic. Cut short. Then starting again. Then cut short. Then starting again. If you can do that, you can master that song, I said to her. And she did. She has performed my *Goat*

Songs all over the world, and wherever she performs them someone in the audience faints, she is so used to it now that she is disappointed if nobody faints. I do not try to beat out the brains of the audience with noise, like some composers, he said. The secret is to be spare with the noise. Spare with everything you do. Each note is a world, Massimo, each sound a universe. I invented a language for Yoko, he said, a language that would allow her to sing as I envisaged her singing. It was such a relief, Massimo, he said, to write in that language, to put my French poetry and my Italian poetry behind me, to feel that it belonged in a different era, to a different person. It belonged to the era of politeness, the era of the waltz in Monte Carlo, of playing at being an artist in London and Vienna and Paris. When I came back from Nepal and shut myself up in the house here in Rome, he said, I knew that I had ceased to play. I knew that I did not have a long time and that there was so much to do, so much to accomplish. The capacity for chaos is always there, he said. If you do not come at things in the right way you will remain on the surface. But if you do not come at things in the right way there is also the possibility that everything will collapse. The Tantric masters knew what they were doing, Massimo, he said. They knew what they were up to. The principle of Tantra, Massimo, he said, is the principle of the retention of the semen. We must reach as close as we can to the sexual climax, he said, but not allow the accumulated tension to explode, as it does in normal sexual intercourse. It must be recycled, he said, so that we can allow the excitement to circulate, if need be for ever. It is a skill which takes many years to master, he said. Western music from Mozart to Mahler, he said, is nothing but delayed gratification ending in consummation and exhaustion. That is the music of adolescents, Massimo, he said. It is the music of adolescent masturbators. Our music has taken a different direction, he said, it has returned to its ancient roots. It has escaped from the puerile imitation of sexual congress, caress, arousal, delay, frenzy, extinction, which was the pattern of Romantic music and the reason for its enormous popularity among the repressed middle classes of Germany and Austria, who imagined that it was leading them up to an aesthetic heaven. Well, he said, they had their climax twice over, first in the First World War and then in the Second World War. That should have been enough for them. But not at all. Look at their books. Look at the music they flock to listen to in the concert halls, this so-called intellectual elite. Caress, arousal, delay, frenzy, extinction. All the same. No change. The basic lesson of history, Massimo, he said, is that no one ever learns the lessons of history. But because no one ever learns the lessons of history, they do not learn this lesson either. By the end he was very weak, sometimes he thought he had been talking to me but it had only been in his head, or his voice was so low that I could not make out what he was saying. As I told you yesterday, Massimo, he would say, and I did not have the heart to tell him he had said nothing the day before. He did not want to see anybody. His agent, Annibale Giacometti, rang every day. He has two great names, Mr Pavone said when I told him, but he himself is not great. In fact he is a dwarf. Spiritually he is a dwarf. His publisher, Herr Groeneboom, from Universal Editions, also rang every day. They do not want the hen that laid the golden eggs to die, he said when I told him. They are vultures, Massimo, vultures. When I am better, he said to me, I want you to drive me to San Felice for one last meal at the

Circeo Park Hotel. My father was a naval officer, Massimo, he said, and I have a longing for the sea. He asked me to read to him the poetry of Montale. His early poetry made a great impression on me, he said. Later he wrote long and soppy poems about love like any other Italian, but his early poems are remarkable. He made me read many poems, 'Ora sia il tuo passo', 'Gloria del disteso mezzogiorno', 'Portami il girasole', and many more. Often he fell asleep as I was reading. He seemed to become very small. He said to me: I will not end my days in a hospital, Massimo, you must make sure that I die here in my house over the Forum. He did not want to see anybody. They will distract me, Massimo, he said, from this, the most important moment of my life. Life is not important, Massimo, he said. What you make of your life is important. And death is important. Just as the most important words in a book are the words of the title, which are written in bigger letters than the rest, so the most important part of life is death, and it is written in bigger letters than the rest of your life. I want to see no one, Massimo, he said. No one. My best hours have been passed alone, Massimo, he said, so why should I at this moment in my life start to see people? But at the funeral there were many people. So many people, sir, you have no idea. His uncle Alessandro, the bishop; his uncle Giacinto, the senator; his cousin Tarquinio, the banker; his cousin Florinda, the actress; his cousin Antonio, the professor; his cousin Giuseppe, the polar explorer; all their wives and their husbands and their children. Also friends and many composers. I do not give a damn for religion, Massimo, he said, but if they want to give me a full Christian burial, that is their right. While I am alive, he said, I belong to myself. When I am dead I will belong to them. I walked with Annamaria at the back. Some of the time I almost had to carry her, she was so frail and crying so much. The dear man, she kept saying, the dear man. Why she said that I do not know. He had often been harsh to her. Especially in the last years, when she could not see so well and she often left marks of dirt on the walls, on the tables. I must sack that woman, he said to me. She is driving me mad with her increasing sloppiness. I must find a good old people's home for her and put her in it and bring in a younger, stronger woman, a woman who is not half-blind and does not dribble all the time, to look after me. But he never did. He said to me, I am tired, Massimo, tired. I have never been tired in my life, but now I am tired. Perhaps it is time to take a rest. Why are you crying, Massimo? he said, I have provided for you in my will. Do not fear. You are not so young yourself, he said, you probably want a bit of a rest yourself. I have provided for you and for Annamaria. You will burn all the shoes, he said, and all the suits and all the shirts and all the ties. Everything is to be burned, he said. I have provided enough for you not to be tempted to take this little thing or that. My family will deal with the rest, he said, and Federico will set up the Foundation, either here or elsewhere. It is of no importance but Federico is keen for it to be established. What do I care? he said. Let them do what they like. I have always done what I liked, why should they not do what they like when I am no longer there? We were visiting the Etruscan necropolis at Cerveteri, walking down the grassy tracks between the tombs. He walked very slowly, leaning on his stick, he would never lean on me. He said to me: Massimo, the most important thing in life is to know what you want to do and then to do it. From as far back as I can remember, he said, I have wanted to make music, so the first half of my life was a mixture of frustration, rage, excitement and depression, because I wanted to make music but I did not know what kind of music it was I wanted to make or how to make it. But when I came back from my trip with Tucci to Nepal, he said, all the anger and frustration had gone and I could sit down and work as I had been put into the world to work. Of course there were still moments of frustration, I will not say it was all plain sailing, there were whole days and even weeks or months when I could not see my way forward, he said, but sooner or later I found the way again. Sound is a creative force, Massimo, he said. Sound is immutable and sound itself is a creative force. My string quartets, he said, are the nearest thing to an account of my feelings I wished to give. Because the quartet has always been associated with inwardness, with feeling, he said. The directions of the Third Quartet are very explicit, he said. First: *Avec une grande tendresse.* Then: *L'appel de l'ésprit, l'homme se réveille.* The final movement: *Libération, catharsis.* But of course I am not Beethoven, he said, nor do I want to be. So I treat all four instruments as one, a giant instrument of sixteen strings. Only the Ardittis play it as it should be played, he said, as at once the most personal and the most impersonal of all my works. I had to help him down the steps, since his fall he had lost confidence in his legs, but he still wanted to see things and he still walked by himself in the streets of Rome at night when he could not sleep and he could not work. There is something about walking in a city in the middle of the night, he said, not in the districts where the bars and nightclubs stay open all night, where the prostitutes walk the streets, but in the residential districts, where every good citizen has gone to sleep, there is something about that, he said, about padding through those quiet residential streets, that I find conducive both to peace of mind and to the emergence of compositional ideas. Perhaps it is because you are in a sense both there and not there, you are already your own ghost, he said, when I am gone I will probably still walk the streets of Rome at night as I have always done, but in a spirit of peace, not of frustration and anguish, as poor benighted Christians think, who worry about holding their dead down in their graves and imagine that if they walk the streets after they are dead and buried it is because they are restless and unappeased. I am not restless when I walk the streets at night, he said. I am never less restless than in those hours. We were standing in the dark in one of the Etruscan tombs. The Etruscans loved silence, he said, and they loved the dark. So it is not surprising that the Romans condemned them to silence and to darkness. The Romans were the most unimaginative people who ever lived, he said. Thank God I am a Sicilian and not a Roman. If I had been a Roman I would never have achieved anything, he said. Everything that is wrong with the human race, he said, can be found in the Romans. They were petty. They were pedantic. They were mean. They were bureaucratic. They were vain. They were bloodthirsty. They were cruel. The Roman roads were straight, he said. The Romans prided themselves on their straight roads. But who wants a straight road? The Romans substituted the straight line for the circle and the spiral, he said. For the Celtic circle and the Celtic spiral they substituted the straight line. And because the Roman road brought peace and prosperity, because along the Roman road other peoples could be subjugated and their wealth taken away, all those who followed the Romans tried to ape the Roman ways. They abandoned the circle and the spiral and became obsessed with the straight line. What is the landing on the moon but the Roman road? What is America but the Roman road? What is the dream of living to a hundred but the Roman road? Capitalism is the Roman road, he said. Communism is the Roman road, and Fascism was the Roman road. One of the joys of travelling in Nepal, he said, and it was one of the joys of travelling in West Africa in my youth, was that there were no Roman roads. The roads led from village to village, and from village to temple. What is the shape of a Buddhist shrine, Massimo? he said. Circular. Darkness is circular, he said. Just as light is circular and each sound is circular. And not circular in two dimensions but in three or four or five, and a circle in four dimensions is a spiral. And what is a spiral but a figure of eight? And what is the sign for infinity but a figure of eight lying on its side? Not only is each of my works a sphere, he said as we stood in the dark of the tomb at Cerveteri, but each moment in each work is a sphere. Those who are willing to listen to my music, he said, learn to listen to all sound. They learn to listen to the reverberations of a sound, to its inner heart. My wife left me in 1945, Massimo, he said to me. One day she was there and the next she was gone. But my other bride, sound, has never left me. Sometimes I have left her. I have been too distracted, too superficial, too frail to stay with her and be her spouse. But she has never left me. Never, Massimo. And she will never leave me. *Elle ne me quittera jamais.* I will leave her, Massimo, he said, but she will never leave me. When you are alive, Massimo, he said, you are a person. When you are dead you are a piece of meat. If it amuses them to make a fuss over a piece of meat, he said, then that is their prerogative. Why should I deny them? I do not want to leave my body to science, he said. I want to leave it to my family to do with as they like. My father is buried in the family vault, Massimo, he said, though he was a freethinker. My mother likewise. If they want to bury me there beside them, let them do so. If they want to cut me into little pieces and throw me into the Tiber, then that too is all right by me. What was good enough for Orpheus is good enough for me, he said. Sometimes he spoke so low that I had to bend over his bed to hear him. Even then I did not always understand what he said. He was not talking to me but to himself. Or perhaps to some imaginary person. But he was very clear that I should not take, even as a memento, anything from his wardrobe. All that has to be burned, he said. He had always been superstitious. When the barber came to cut his hair he always insisted that every last hair should be gathered up from the floor and burned. When he cut his nails he always made sure the cuttings were swept up and disposed of. If a black cat crossed the road he would not go on. Turn the car, Massimo, he would say. There is nothing for it but to go home. If I suggested an alternative route he would pretend to consider it and then say he was really too tired, it had not been a good idea to set out in the first place and he only wanted to return. If he saw a new moon through the car window he would say: It is a bad sign, Massimo, a very bad sign. Who knows what disaster is about to befall me? If I made the mistake of pointing out, after a few days, that no disaster had struck, he would say, Patience, Massimo, patience. Ill fortune is often slow to arrive, but, believe me, arrive it will. Storms terrified him. I found him one day, when I came up to take my orders and thunder was cracking right overhead as if the gods were moving house, and the lightning seemed to be streaking straight down to the

Forum, I found him hiding under the table, the round table by the armchair. I pretended I had not seen him and after looking round the room went on my way. But I made sure after that not to take him out for a drive if storms were forecast, even if it was bright sunshine. I would explain that something had gone wrong with the car and it would not be fit for the roads in time. When his dear friend Henri Michaux died, his funeral took place in driving rain, the thunder rumbled overhead. I knew what an effort it was for him to turn out, but he did not say a word. It was only later, as we were driving back to Rome, that he said to me: Did you hear the thunder, Massimo? Even the gods were angry that Henri had died. I will write a piece in his memory, he said. I do not know what form it will take but I know that I will write something. Writing will be better than crying, he said. It will be better than feeling his absence all the time like a wound in my body. Writing it will allow me to live with him and talk to him, even though he is no longer there. I knew a great many people in Paris in those years before and after the war, he said to me, some, like René Daumal, remarkable, others, like Jean-Paul Sartre and Mme Pierre Jean Jouve, frightful. I had friends among the *clochards* on the banks of the Seine and I had friends among the poets, I even had friends among the upper echelons of the Church and would frequently dine with industrialists and bankers. It always amazed me, he said, that the poets only knew other poets and the bankers other bankers. We must mingle with all and sundry, Massimo, he said, that is the only way to live. It was René Daumal who first suggested I go to India, who first drew my attention to the mystical traditions of India and Tibet. He was a very remarkable man. But he was not a friend in the way Henri was a friend.

I have had three real friends in my life, he said. There was Daniel Bernstein, when I was young, with whom I went climbing in the Alps and then to West Africa and to Egypt. He died of TB in 1937, which saved him from witnessing the destruction of his entire family in the following years. There was Henri Michaux. And there was another, whom I have forgotten. I have of course had many close and valuable relationships with those who performed my music, with a very few composers, with Tucci, who was another remarkable man, and Fosco Maraini. And then there were the Nepalese guides, he said, men of few words and deep faith. Meeting them and being in their company day and night for several months was almost as important for me as seeing their extraordinary country and hearing their music. There is no music like it, Massimo, he said to me, experiencing their music made me realise with a renewed force what little *weight* sound has for composers in our Western tradition. Sound can be beautiful, it can be loud, it can be soft, it can be abrasive, but it lacks weight, Massimo, sound in our Western tradition lacks weight. Even Bach, he said, who loved a beautiful melody and whose mind could solve the most abstruse musical and mathematical conundrums, even he could not help but take sound itself too lightly. He could not help it, he said, he was a man of his time. Only in Gregorian chant, he said, can you hear something of the density in each sound that you will hear in a Nepalese Buddhist temple. But only in the solemn trumpets in a Nepalese temple, high up in the mountains, do you really come close to the core of sound, the molten lava that lies boiling away in every sound as it does in the recesses of the earth. No wonder the temple musicians must train for years, not just musically but spiritually, before they dare to let loose on those trumpets. If you are not prepared, not spiritually and mentally prepared, Massimo, he said, you will be annihilated. Annihilated. It is the same with everything. If you are not prepared you are annihilated. Not physically, of course, though physical annihilation is always a possibility, but spiritually and mentally. Most of those you see walking around you every day. Massimo, he said, have been annihilated in this way. They have been lobotomised. They have been castrated. By their parents. By their schooling, By their wives. By their friends. By their employers. That is the world we live in, Massimo, he said. We have to recognise it and then to rise above it. It is our duty to ourselves in the first place, but also to the world which brought us forth, as we are, ourselves and no one else. When we die, Massimo, he said, and St Peter asks us what we have to say for ourselves, all we need to say is that we have been ourselves and no one else. If you are truly yourself, he said, you will speak for everyone. If you are not yourself you cannot blow that trumpet, Massimo, he said. That trumpet will defeat you. That is why it requires years and years of training, to empty yourself out, to purify yourself, until you are ready to blow the trumpet. When I am gone, he said, if you chance to listen to my music, it will perhaps give you a hint of what I am talking about. My Foundation will keep my works in print and make sure they are performed and recorded, he said. It is Federico's brainchild. I have no interest in it. In the old days, Massimo, he said, they built chantry chapels and paid for monks to say prayers there in perpetuity, so that their souls could be eased through the difficult journey of Purgatory. Nowadays they set up Foundations so as to keep their memories alive and their noses visible in the world. I do not want my memory to be kept alive, he said, but I am too tired to fight them. I know that my music will survive as long as music is performed, and that is enough for me. Or perhaps it will not. Who is to say, Massimo? What my trip to Nepal taught me, he said, is that we have to live in the present, difficult as that is. They closed the streets for the funeral, you should have seen the procession, sir, all those cardinals and judges and the rest of them and the Sicilian nobles he despised and all the people he knew, for a man who prided himself on his isolation from the world he had made friends with a great many people, maybe on his walks through Rome at night he befriended them, gypsies and black people and Indians and all sorts, I did not know there were so many different races living in Rome. It is among the outcasts and the reviled, he said, that you will most often find true spirituality. He despised the new Sicilian nobles. They are all bankers or ne'er-do-wells, he said. They think the world owes them a living just because they are born into a noble family. The best of them are simple, the result of too much inbreeding over the centuries, and the worst are crooks who should be behind bars, and many of them are. They are no better than the Mafia, he said, and often they actually are the Mafia. This country cannot be cleaned up, Massimo, he said. It is corrupt through and through and it does not have the will to change itself and to make a clean sweep of it. That does not stop me loving it, and especially this city of Rome, he said. I could have lived anywhere but I chose to live here in Rome, he said. For here we are truly at the centre of the earth, at the meeting-place of east and west, north and south. Do you know what they say about Naples? he said to me one day. We were driving out into the Campagna in the evening and not going anywhere in particular, as he liked to do some-

times to help him think about his music. They say, he said, that
Naples is the only Third World city without a European
quarter. Rome will never turn into that, he said. Naples and
Rome are as different as chalk and cheese. Sometimes he sat
beside me without talking for the whole drive. I don't believe
he was thinking about his music any more. Sometimes he was
just dozing. The windows were shut and the air conditioning
was on, it was too hot even at that time of day to open the
windows. He did not bother to direct me, to tell me where he
wanted to go. I kept to the quiet roads, the smaller roads,
through villages and fields. Sometimes he made me stop and
would get out to relieve himself or just to stand at the edge of
a field and listen to the cicadas. They were singing before
mankind ever came on the scene, he said, and they will go on
singing long after we have all passed away. I sat in the car with
the door open and sometimes he stood there for half an hour
at a time, leaning on his stick and just looking across the fields.
He stayed in Rome throughout the summer, August in Rome
is the best month, Massimo, he said. The locals flee to the hills
and the sea, the tourists avoid it. It is a city emptied of people,
emptied of its traffic. I have always done my best work in the
summer, he said, I have always found the summer conducive to
good work. Sometimes he would ask me to get out of the car
and walk a few steps with him. He would walk a little and then
sit down at the edge of a wood or a field. He would hold out
his hand and stick out a finger. Listen, Massimo, he would say.
Listen to the sound the air makes as it comes into contact with
my hand. Do you hear it, Massimo? he would say, and if I said
no sometimes he would get angry and shout and tell me that I
needed to have my ears cleaned, that they were full of Roman

filth. So I usually said yes, that I could hear it, even when I couldn't. What sound does it make, Massimo? he would say, and I would say: Like a wave, and that would please him. Yes, he would say, there are waves everywhere, not just in the sea, there are waves of sound and waves of light. The idea of the wave, he said to me once, as we were driving again, is the idea of life itself. That is what Heraclitus meant, he said, when he said that when I step into a river I do not step into the river and it is not me that steps into it. To write music that is and is not static, that is and is not in motion, that both sounds and is silent, that goes inwards and that goes backwards and that does not go anywhere at all, that is the idea, he said, that is what I have tried to do for the past thirty years. I did not wish to write music that was profound, he said. I did not wish to write music that was beautiful. I did not wish to write music that would make audiences clap and agents come rushing up to me to sign me up to go to this festival or that festival. I wanted to write music that was true. True to our earth. True to our planet. And if it is true it will be frightening. It does not have to be loud to be frightening, he said. When I used a double bass and the voice, that was frightening enough. People have told me that when they heard my *Ongamak*, which is what this piece was called, they wanted to run away, they wanted to bury themselves in the earth. The music of the pygmies of central Africa, he said, and the music of the Katchak or Monkey Dance of Bali, and the music of the temples of Nepal and Tibet, these musics do not try to be profound and they do not try to be beautiful, Massimo, he said, they do not try to be anything. They are what they are, Massimo, he said. *Ils ne sont que ce qu'ils sont.* The world is being swallowed up in superficiality, Massimo, he said to me, and the artists and intellectuals react to this by seeking profundity. When they grow tired of profundity they play ironically with superficiality. But they are wrong on both counts. They should not seek the depths and they should not seek the surfaces, they should seek the truth. We were allowed to pay our last respects, me and Annamaria, he said, the family allowed us to stand in the room where he lay. Annamaria was crying and holding my hand. His cheeks had sunk right in so that the bones were visible, with the skin stretched tight over them. They had not yet shaved him and his chin was covered with a fine white down. I remembered when I had carried him from the car in his blanket to sit at the edge of the forest, on one of our last outings. He weighed hardly anything. You could see the outline of his body under the sheet. I remembered what he had said to me many times: The body is nothing, Massimo, the spirit is all. What is music, Massimo, he said, except the triumph of the spirit? Even sex, he said, even sex is the triumph of the spirit. It is not the triumph of the flesh, he said, it is the triumph of the spirit. I learned this when I first learned about sex, he said, when my little cousin let me pass my hand over her lovely young breast. It was not so much the feel of her breast, he said, the feel of her firm young breast under my hand, as the sense that it was her breast I was touching, a secret part of her I was being allowed to touch. A strange ritual was being enacted, Massimo, he said, a ritual in which a magical union was being cemented. My wife did not understand this, he said. For her sex was sex and that was it, which means that for her it was nothing at all. Music is like a woman, Massimo, he said. You have to woo it and you have to be infinitely patient with it and in the end you have to recognise that you may think you have reached the heart of the sound but it will always elude you. You may hit upon a means of expressing it, but you yourself will never fully grasp what it is you have done. We sat at the edge of the wood. Night was falling but the cicadas were in full voice. I thought perhaps he had gone to sleep. He did sometimes and then I had to wait till he woke up and asked to be taken home. But then he spoke. I could not see his face because of the way he was sitting. Listen to their music, he said. Listen to the throbbing power of it. Where is the Greek or the Italian composer who has responded to this powerful music, which is, after all, there for all to hear? A few Renaissance composers seem to have been interested in cicadas. Stefano Landi wrote a madrigal about a cicada singing as it dies, and Monteverdi made a little joke out of humans imitating cicadas in one of his madrigals, he said, a delightful joke, but a joke nonetheless. But the demonic power of the song of the cicada has remained untapped by musicians. And yet when you listen to it, it is as powerful in its way as anything you will hear coming out of a Buddhist temple in Nepal or Tibet. And what is it saying, Massimo? What is it saying? *Now*, it is saying, and *eternity*. If you can hear the *now*, he said, you can hear eternity. That is what I have tried to do, he said, to write a music of now which would be a music of eternity. Then he was silent for a long time. Then he said: Take me home, Massimo. I wanted to hear the cicadas for one last time and now I have heard them. I gathered him up in his blanket. Though he gave the impression in his prime of being such a tall man, he was in actual fact of average height, and at the end he weighed very little. He did not move and he did not speak. All the way home I sensed that the end was near but I did not want to think about it. Annamaria had made a soup but he would not touch it. Take me to bed, he said to me. Take me to bed and put out the light and then leave me. When I laid him down he said to me: When I was a child the kitchen girls put me to bed. I felt at ease with them as I never felt with my mother. I am telling you so much that you do not understand, Massimo, he said. But it does me good to talk. Sometimes I did not catch what he was saying, he spoke very low, and though I bent towards him I could not always distinguish the words. Also, since his stroke, he sometimes spoke in a blurred way. And sometimes the breath in his throat was louder than any of the words he spoke, if you know what I mean, sir. Sometimes he became angry if I or someone else did not understand him, he would scream and talk faster and that made it even more difficult. Then he would bang the door of his room and bang the windows and we would hear him walking up and down, up and down. The Arditti Quartet were working with him on a recording of all his quartets and sometimes he shouted at them because they did not understand what he said. It was difficult for everybody, but most of all for Mr Pavone himself, of course. Then there were times when he spoke quite clearly. Low but quite clearly. He would ask me to drive him out just as in the old days and often he would talk. I had the misfortune to be born in the early years of the century, Massimo, he said, so that I can consider myself a child of the century. You were born in the middle of the century, so that you will have the chance to live in two centuries, but I am stuck with this one. Has there ever been a worse century, Massimo? he said. One in which more planned and premeditated murder and destruction has ever taken place? Human beings are always keen to kill and destroy each other, he said, but they have never had the means to do so in such numbers until this century. And yet in the midst of all this carnage I have led a charmed life, he said. I have done what I wanted to do and also what I had to do. I have lived daily and even hourly with my beloved music, he said, and I have explored its secrets and been touched by its beneficent power. I sometimes ask myself what would have happened to me if I had not gone to Nepal when I did, he said, but then I have realised that everything in my life had led up to that decision. I went when I did because that was when I was ready to go. I did not go before because before I was not ready. It is as simple as that, Massimo, he said. After my trip, he said, everything fell into place. Instead of fighting the darkness I settled down in the darkness. Instead of trying to rise above the body, as that idiot Scheler had tried to get me to do, I settled down inside my body. When I came back from Nepal and shut myself up in the house here in Rome, he said, I knew that I had ceased to play. I knew that I did not have a long time and that there was so much to do, so much to accomplish. I have been blessed, Massimo, he said, blessed. I found a way to stop playing at being an artist, I found a way to return to myself and to leave myself behind in my work. Mr Salvatore called me after the funeral and said to me: The Count has made provision for you in his will, Massimo, but if you would like to work for the Foundation, I am sure we would be able to find a niche for you. I told him I was not interested in working for the Foundation. I understand, Massimo, he said. You would like to spread your wings. I told him that, having worked for Mr Pavone for all these years I could not bear to stay in his house when he was no longer there. It is his music we have to think about, he said. It is his music he would have wanted us to think about, not himself. I told him I appreciated that but I was not someone who understood about music. I had been hired to look after Mr Pavone and his clothes and to drive him. You know how it is, sir. If you should ever change your mind, Massimo, he said, just give me a ring. We could use someone like you, Massimo, he said. The Count always spoke highly of you, he said. Despite that early incident concerning Miss Mauss, he always spoke highly of you. I asked him what he meant but he only said, you know what I am talking about, Massimo. Nothing was ever proved, I said. You are quite right, Massimo, he said. Besides, this is not the moment to rake over these old embers. So I have not returned, sir, I took my things and left the house for ever. That is what Mr Pavone would have wanted. When I am gone you will still have much of your life left to live, Massimo, he said. I shall make sure you are well provided for, but after that you are on your own. When Arabella left for the last time, at the end of the war, he said, I sat in my room for twenty-four hours and I did not move. Then I tried to live in Paris again. I could not bear to remain in Switzerland or to return to Rome. I wanted a change. And I had many friends in Paris. First I stayed with Henri Michaux and with Ronaldo, his cat. His wife had died after a long illness and he was inconsolable, so he was not a very good companion, but Ronaldo was a great comfort to me. A great comfort. He was a character. Much more intelligent than his master. Not as good a poet and painter, but much more intelligent. I wonder how different my life would have been had I lived with a cat, he said. Ronaldo had six toes on three of his four feet and seven on one, and he spent a great deal of time licking and cleaning them. The flat was filthy, Michaux refused to have anyone come in to clean it, but Ronaldo was a little island of cleanliness in an ocean of filth. It was only

Ronaldo's presence that kept me from moving, he said. In the end I did move, and though I called on Henri almost every day and spent many hours with Ronaldo, it was no longer the same thing. If only human beings were as self-contained and undemanding as cats, Massimo, he said, marriage would be a much more successful institution. But human beings are not self-contained. Women in particular need constant reassurance. I lived for several months with a beautiful young woman in Monte Carlo, he said. She was a gifted singer but she had no self-confidence. She wanted to be told all the time that she was a great singer, and also that she was a beautiful woman. How many beautiful women have been great singers or great painters or great writers, Massimo? When you are beautiful you do not need to make the effort, everything is given to you, yet without great effort you cannot become great at anything. But when we are young we want everything. We want to be beautiful and a great singer, beautiful and a great artist. It is folly, Massimo, folly. Finally she said to me: You do not appreciate my art, Tancredo. You have no real desire for me. You do not really love me. I am a token, she said. A beautiful bird you are happy to have trapped. Let me tell you, Tancredo, she said, I am stifling here. Stifling. It was a relief when she was gone, Massimo, he said. A great relief. Whereas Ronaldo rolled over on his back and purred when I stroked his stomach, and when he had had enough he simply got to his feet and moved away. We have to return to the simplicity and the immediacy of animals, Massimo, he said. Our art has to be able to stand up and walk away if it wants to. Or lie down and allow its stomach to be tickled. It was perhaps Ronaldo who prepared me for Nepal, he said. I did not realise it at the time, but afterwards I understood. I understood too that he had come into my life at a particular moment and that it would never do to try and replicate the experience here in Rome. Everything is changing, Massimo, he said. The Neolithic age is coming to an end. What we called civilisation is coming to an end. Composers go on composing and posing for photographers in their studies and appearing at festivals, but it is all coming to an end. Everybody thinks that with a few bombs they can manage to change the world, but what they don't realise is that the world is changing, whether they like it or not. Soon Communism and also capitalism will collapse, Massimo, they will implode because of the contradictions in the system. I am fortunate that I was able to work as I did, he said, between the end of the world wars and the end of civilisation. It has been a period of calm, Massimo, he said. A period of relative calm. At least for us in the West. The people of Tibet have been hounded out of their country and brutalised, he said, and the pygmies of central Africa have been more or less wiped out. Age-old cultures are disappearing every day. Whole languages are disappearing every day. They now have exhibitions of the art of Benin in the most prestigious museums in the world, in New York, in London, in Paris, but the art of the Ife and of Benin is disappearing. We were the fortunate ones, Massimo, he said to me. We were able to go to Benin and also to Nepal and to see the living art and the living culture, but of course the fact that we could go was also the sign that these cultures were coming to an end. Africa is full of anthropological museums, he said, and that is the sign that Africa has died. A living culture has turned into a dead culture. This happened in Europe in the Renaisssance, he said. A few monks go on singing the Gregorian chant, he said, but the tradition is no longer alive. It is up to each of us to find that which is alive in each tradition, and to breathe new life into it. I have no illusions such as Schoenberg had that I have in any way advanced the cause of music. But that is not the point. That was never the point, Massimo, he said. When you are in touch with sound, with the innermost heart of sound, then such notions as art and music, advance and decline, past and future, good and bad, beautiful and ugly cease to make sense. It becomes a question of being open, Massimo, of listening, and of daring. I learned to fear nothing on my parents' estate all those years ago, Massimo, he said. I learned it climbing trees and making love to the servant girls deep down inside their giant beds in which five of them slept together. I learned it when I was allowed to attack the pianos that filled the house as they needed to be attacked, head on, banging the lid, running my hands through their insides and listening to the noise it made, just as I pushed my hands into all the available orifices of the serving girls and listened, deep down under the blankets, to their sighs and their moans. There must be no fear, Massimo, he said, no fear in the face of life and no fear in the face of death. We sat in the car looking out at the landscape, it was cold, he did not want to get out, often I could not hear what he said, but he went on talking, paying no attention to me, looking out, the sky was grey, there was even snow in the air, when he stopped I did not know if he wanted me to drive on, I stayed as still as I could, he was so used to me it was as if he was alone, I could make out a few words, Monte Carlo, Ronaldo, Jouve, Kang Shi, something like that, once after he had been silent for a long time I asked him if he wanted me to drive him home, I was afraid he would catch cold, with the engine off the car was like a fridge, he didn't reply, his lips were blue, finally I started the car and he said nothing and while I drove he said nothing. I was thinking of our other drives, over the years, mainly in the summer and spring, I was thinking of how many more hours I had spent with him in the car than in any other situation, I would never have imagined it when I first went to work for him but that is how it turned out, we never know what will happen, we can never predict. I thought, when he is gone I will remember sitting in the car with him better than I remember anything else and I thought I would often dream after he was gone that he was sitting beside me in the big car and I was driving him through the Roman Campagna and if I didn't dream, I thought, then I would certainly think it, especially every time I drove a car, it would certainly be there in my head the way things stay in your head and then I thought, I suppose when I too am gone it will not be in anybody's head, but that will not matter, as Mr Pavone always said, it is the music that matters, Massimo, not you and me but the music, on the other hand you have to ask yourself where the music would have been if Mr Pavone had not been there to compose it, you have to ask yourself that, yes, sir, you have to ask yourself that.

He was silent.

I waited for him to continue.

When it became clear that he was not going to, I said: Go on.

– I have nothing more to say, sir, he said.

– Would you like to rest? I asked him.

– No, sir, he said.

– Would you like us to go on tomorrow?

– No, sir, he said. I have nothing more to say.

— Are you quite sure?

— Yes, sir, he said.

— Then all that remains is for me to thank you, I said.

— Yes, sir, he said. Thank you, sir.

THE END

Note

The protagonist of this novel is loosely based on the Italian composer Giacinto Scelsi (1905–1988). The author would like to thank the Fondazione Isabella Scelsi, Rome, for permission to incorporate fragments from Scelsi's own writings into the narrative.